KISS OF THE BEGGAR

PROSE SERIES 74

Canada Council for the Arts

Conseil des Arts du Canada

ONTARIO ARTS COUNCIL
CONSEIL DES ARTS DE L'ONTARIO

Guernica Editions Inc. acknowledges the support of The Canada Council for the Arts.
Guernica Editions Inc. acknowledges the support of the Ontario Arts Council.

PIERRE L'ABBÉ

KISS OF THE BEGGAR

SHORT STORIES

GUERNICA

TORONTO – BUFFALO – CHICAGO – LANCASTER (U.K.)

2005

The Kiss previously appeared in
Your Baggage Is in Buffalo (Hamilton Artists Inc., 1994)

Antonio D'Alfonso, editor
Guernica Editions Inc.
P.O. Box 117, Station P, Toronto (ON), Canada M5S 2S6
2250 Military Road, Tonawanda, N.Y. 14150-6000 U.S.A.

Distributors:
University of Toronto Press Distribution,
5201 Dufferin Street, Toronto (ON), Canada M3H 5T8
Gazelle Book Services, White Cross Mills, High Town, Lancaster LA1 1XS U.K.
Independent Publishers Group,
814 N. Franklin Street, Chicago, Il. 60610 U.S.A.

First edition.
Printed in Canada.

Legal Deposit – Fourth Quarter
National Library of Canada
Library of Congress Catalog Card Number: 2005931739
Library and Archives Canada Cataloguing in Publication
L'Abbé, Pierre, 1959-
Kiss of the beggar / Pierre L'Abbé.
(Prose series ; 74)
ISBN 1-55071-230-6
I. Title. II. Series.
PS8573.A155K58 2005   C813'.54   C2005-905219-8

CONTENTS

FOR MARY ANNE

Robert was fixing his tie. He pulled it up tight. He liked a nice fit. This set him apart at the Institute. Everyone else was lax or boring. He undid his belt and readjusted his shirt. His drop-shoulder short sleeves, at least, made a statement. He would have to get some new ones when they visited New Zealand at Christmas. The collar was crisp; he tugged at it. Joan had the daughters of one of the secretaries at the Institute iron them; the girls starched them up nice.

Joan had come in and was rustling about behind him. He found it bothersome when he was standing at the mirror. He put on his black jacket with the rounded lapels and did a couple windmills to settle the shoulders into place. He cut quite the figure in the corridors of the Institute with his tall slender physique and his light curly hair. Everyone respected his research there; it was respected around the world. If he started coming into work looking like everyone else, they would think his research was falling off.

There was no letting up for a future Director. Robert was still young and Ragomolli's tenure was up in two years. Robert would have a chance though if Rag managed to get his own position extended for another two years. Who else was there anyway? It couldn't be anyone from the laboratory side because Rag was from there. His own chief was a nice guy, but the higher-ups were already coming straight to Robert. The other chiefs were goofs and imps. The only problem was his squash buddy, Thompson. But Thompson, prick that he was, was already assuming he was in and was making enemies fast. Robert could capitalize on that.

Robert practised curling his upper lip the way he would

when Dr. Darby said: "Robert, you look so dashing this morning," or "Robert, you look so darned handsome today." If the curled-up lip wasn't enough for Annette, he'd give her his sour smile, then start listing annual risk estimates for childhood leukaemia at the nuclear site in Scotland, and ask her if she had verified them. If he left now he'd be able to grab Darby and go the Au Coin for a *café très serré* and be back in time to bump into Ragomolli when he was going into the Chiefs' meeting at 10:15. And that way Robert could be seen coming into the building with Darby.

He was going to have to do a better job of convincing Annette that the favours were all coming from him. "Let's go to the Au Coin," he'd say. "Too many spies around here." He'd lean over the table and speak in a snarly low voice, "Thompson wants to get his hands on these liver studies." She'd believe him too, because she was always going on about how Thompson was trying to get his hands on everything. "If Rag wasn't on side, I might have lost them already. I'm only giving them to you because you have to make your mark." She'd really pour it on then. "Oh, Robert, I don't know what I'd do if I didn't have a friend in this place." At that point, she'd probably touch his arm, the little over-achiever.

Robert was acting agitated as though he was ready to leave. It was a little early Joan thought. He often went into work late.

"What are you smiling at, Robert?"

They saw one another in the mirror. "Ragomolli. I've got a meeting with him this morning. Wants me to get a couple studies away from Thompson."

"Oh," Joan answered.

Joan followed Robert out of the bedroom. She really needed to talk to him. She thought perhaps he could take her to drop the kids, then they could go for coffee. She wasn't dressed yet, but that was no problem. She could slip into something and tie back her hair.

"Do you have time to go for coffee, Robert?"

Robert looked at his watch. "The kids aren't ready."

Joan's heart sank. She knew from his voice there would be no convincing him.

"I'll kiss you now then." Joan laid a hand on Robert's chest and closed her eyes.

"Mip, don't look so pained when you kiss Robert."

"Sarah, I don't look pained."

"You do, Mippy."

"Sarah."

Joan picked up Mark's hat and coat from the floor. She wanted to hide from Robert. This "Mippy and Dippy" and "Robert and Joan" business had to stop, no matter what Robert thought.

When Robert was gone, Joan leaned against the door and took a deep breath. She had no idea she looked "pained" when she kissed her husband. Afraid of how she must look, she closed her eyes and imagined the scene over again. But when her eyes shut, she saw Robert kissing Annette in bed – Robert kissing Annette in the car.

Joan pushed Mark out the door while trying to manage Bobby in the stroller with her hip.

Sarah was at the elevator, "Are you finally coming, Mip?"

"Sarah," Joan froze.

Madame Destroisfleurs came out of her apartment with her daughter. Three and a half years they had been neighbours and Joan still didn't know the woman's first name. Joan was digging in her bag for the key. She could see Madame Destroisfleurs' shiny shoes, her impeccable skirt. Having found the key Joan decided to dig a little longer until Madame D. said: "Bonjour Madame," and Joan could answer, "Bonjour Madame," and so with the formalities over the woman would be on her way. But the shoes weren't moving. Joan gave in and looked up. Madame Destroisfleurs was shaking her head. The woman's tight-fitting vest, her high-necked laced collar, the set hair and the child in a triple-skirted dress.

"Si votre mari n'était pas médecin . . ."

"I know, I know," Joan answered sarcastically in English, "I wouldn't be able to dress like this." She was going to explain once again that her husband "est docteur, mais pas médecin," but thought it better to let the woman wallow in her ignorance. She knew it was an affront to the neighbours to go out with one of Robert's work shirts draped over her spandex slacks. But hell, she had good legs for forty.

Down on the street, Joan took Sarah over a couple blocks to within site of the school and sent her on her way. Joan then set off with Mark and Bobby on her usual detour. She was going to check on Rag's car. She hated to think of herself as a gossip, but how much excitement could she get ferrying her kids back and forth from school. She was just in time. There was more to garner than Joan had counted on. Down a couple blocks, she could make out Yvonne's petite figure on the step leaning out to kiss Rag. He had a hand on her backside. They were coming out of the Institute's apartment, which everyone referred to Yvonne's place. Rag often stayed there, leaving his teenagers to fend for themselves out in Côte des Sources. Luigina, his wife, lived in Milan. The first time Joan met Luigina was at a summer place Robert had rented from a colleague. Joan had told her guests, many of whom only knew Rag to see him, that he would be coming with his friend, Yvonne. When the tall elegant wife, Luigina, showed up, she answered politely in perfect French or English to everyone who addressed her as Yvonne. She didn't correct anyone once, and for that matter, neither did Rag.

When Yvonne started coming down the sidewalk toward her, Joan quickly wheeled the stroller around and crossed the street. She was entering the rue du 4 Septembre. For a moment she considered going down another block to avoid the *clochard*, but this was the quickest route and the idea that some dirty old man should make her go out of her way bothered her. For months she had been passing him. Today at least, she was on the other side of the street and would not have to wheel the stroller off the sidewalk. In a way, she admired his dedication – he was always awake at this time. She had never seen anyone try to move in on his territory as often happened with the beggars at the post-office. Perhaps he had carved out his own niche in the begging world with a clientele of parents.

Joan never gave him anything because of the way he looked at her. She thought he was leering, but it was hard to tell if the desire in his eyes was for her, or money, or drink. She thought he made forward remarks. But he was always mumbling and the way the French could be insulting with a tone of civility made deciphering his intent all the more difficult. She thought if she had given him a little something at the beginning he would have been more polite. She wasn't against what he was doing. God knows, she had even panhandled herself back in the psychedelic days.

After she dropped Mark at the *maternelle*, Joan wound her way back to their local café where she and Robert often took their morning coffee. The workmen watched from the bar as she tried to hold the door and drag the stroller up the step. She no longer bothered to try the helpless sad eyes or the exasperated look. No one but the patronne of the café would ever move to help her and she came just as Joan managed to get in.

"Votre mari, il s'en vient?"

"Non, pas ce matin." They talked for a moment about the sleeping baby. Joan never ceased to be surprised at her own chatting on this way. Street talk had never been her strong point. The French she had learned from books and teachers was a different kind of language, something lacking any sense of suggestion, a language that never left space for a shrug or that quintessentially French pursing of the lips and jutting of the lower jaw.

Joan ordered a *café crème* and pushed the stroller to her usual seat. Before she sat she leaned over and kissed Bobby. He was so easy, unlike the first two. After his bottle at seven he had slept through being dressed and thrown in the stroller and pushed in the cold to Sarah's school and Mark's *maternelle*. He would wake up soon; these were her last few minutes alone. Yesterday, he had slept past ten and she and Robert had taken a really long coffee. They talked about New Zealand mostly. If she had gone back to the flat instead of coming to the café she might have got in half an hour to work on her story. God, how long had it been since she worked on it – a month? Maybe in the afternoon, if Mark played by himself for a bit while Bobby was napping, she would be able to look at it. Not really work on it, but read it over, do a little editing.

When the *patronne* brought the steaming coffee, Joan hardly remembered where she was. They went through the formalities of the encounter: "Votre café, Madame."

"Merci, Madame."

The forced smiles. As though they had not, just moments ago, chatted in a familial way.

Joan wrapped her hands around the large bowl and held her nose to warm it in the steam. The sweet smell of the hot milk. It was not unlike the odour of the big old collie that guarded the entry to the bar. He slept there all day, only opening his eyes and half lifting his head when a customer came in. Otherwise, he was oblivious to everything, even the *patronne* and her husband stepping over him with tea or coffee.

Joan held the bowl in her finger tips to take a first sip, but she couldn't keep her eyes open. Now the milk smelt unpleasant. She smelt the fish that hadn't been cleaned up. She saw Annette.

The aggravated feeling Joan had woken up with came back. She remembered going to bed that way.

"Not feeling well? I'll clean up." Robert had offered after they had said good-bye to the Darbys. Joan had been miffed after another evening of divided conversation. It was supposed to be a welcome dinner for the new couple, but Annette and her projects, her health, her grandfather's health had seemed more important. After dinner, Robert and Annette had talked Institute politics with the new guy. What was his name – John? A tall, research brain, had never heard of Chagall. His wife was a little better, but had trouble following the conversation between herself and George Darby.

Thank God for George, someone to talk to in this Institute universe. George had tried at first to chat with the new guy – the EEC, the Middle East, climatic zones in Australia. But the John guy simply said, "No, I don't think you understand research," and turned his chair toward Robert and Annette.

This John guy's wife – what *was* her name? – was droning on about how excited she was to be in France. And Joan beaming a big smile, had thought to herself, "What am I doing in this desolate town?" She remembered repeating this phrase to herself and sipping the wine, suggesting the woman try another cheese and wondering, "Do I really think that? Do I really want to get out of here?" She did want to go back to New Zealand – that was always the plan – eventually. But there was Robert and his career to think of. It did make for sense for them to put stock in his career.

When they first came to France the idea was that they would check it out for a few months and then decide. But immediately they got sucked into the new couple tour. After studying French literature all those years, there were so many places Joan wanted to see. On the weekends, they were always off to another historical spot or museum, travelling on trains or driving in rented cars through the country – Robert crazy about taking the corners at ridiculous speeds and she holding her hands folded over her big stomach pregnant with Mark. Everyone loved Sarah and the cute little French phrases Joan had prompted her on. After six months, Robert had started two big cohort studies and it seemed there was no going back. Over the years, she had brought up the issue a few times in company. Robert always supported her and said they would go back, but they never discussed when.

She and Robert were close. They were best friends and discussed everything. It was hard for Joan to admit that any issue had become tabu. So much so that she didn't even want to think that returning to New Zealand was a point of contention. Now, there was another issue Joan hesitated to raise – what were Robert and Annette doing in the car? She didn't even know it bothered her so much until she dropped Bobby.

Joan was holding Bobby in her arms and bouncing him. He had just learned to really laugh. Each time she bounced him she said, "Daddy is coming. Daddy is coming," until he was laughing uncontrollably. She bounced him higher and higher and went over to the window. "Look," she pointed down to the street, "Daddy is coming." She was standing there when their battered old Renault pulled up. Joan waited for Robert to jump out so she could say, "Look, there's Daddy." But when he didn't she leaned over to look down the four stories into the car. She could make out the two figures. Annette was driving and Robert was leaning over her. Their heads weren't visible and neither were Annette's arms. Either her arms were down by the seat or they were around Robert's neck. Joan remembered Robert mentioning that Annette had asked to borrow the car. Maybe he was showing her where the flashers were.

When Robert came up she waited by the window until he was inside before she went to kiss him. While he was taking off his coat she walked up and stretched out her arms and said, "Here's your baby." That's when Bobby fell.

"Oh, I thought you had him," Joan laughed and covered her mouth with her finger tips. She did think he had Bobby. Luckily, Robert was quick enough to catch him.

Joan had turned away, "He needs a bath; he's really filthy."

"What about a kiss," Robert had asked? She returned and stood up on her toes, rubbing her lips against his rough cheek. Then she went into the bathroom, turned on the water and cried.

The next day Joan was sure that Robert had just been showing Annette where the flashers were. It *was* confusing. That was the reason Joan gave for not wanting to drive in France – because the flashers and the shift were screwed up. But then Joan remembered that Annette was American and wouldn't be confused, since the wheel was on the proper side for her.

Joan looked at her watch. She had let her coffee get cold again and Bobby was still asleep. She should have gone home. In a minute, she had gathered her things and left the café. As she sped down the busy street, Bobby sat up in the stroller and twisted about looking at all the cars and people. Joan looked around too. She might see the back of Robert's head or Annette's shoes somewhere in the crowd. But they wouldn't, not in public, not under her nose, not in front of everyone at the Institute. No, they were just good friends. Annette said as much publicly. How else could they be so touchy without everyone thinking something was happening between them.

Joan pushed Bobby into the elevator and hit four. She hated feeling like this and she wasn't going to spend her life being suspicious and bitter. She and Robert were just getting a little out of touch. What they needed was a good talk over dinner. It was too late to get a sitter. She would make dinner. Get some of Robert's favourite things. In the kitchen, she put Bobby on the floor with a piece of cheese and took down the cook books.

On the left side of a piece of paper, she listed courses –
the perfect ones for this time of year: *crudités, soupe, une
plate aux légumes* . . . Then found recipes and jotted down
the ingredients. She could do the shopping on her way
back from picking up Mark. Robert would love it. They
both would. And she would cook all afternoon. There was
just time enough to change Bobby and throw the breakfast
things into the sink.

As she rushed along the street, Joan pulled out the
shopping list and tried to lay out in her mind the stores she
would hit on her way back. She planned a little speech for
Mark: "Mommy is going to be very busy this afternoon.
She has to make a special dinner for Daddy." That sounded stupid she thought; perhaps she would just offer him a
candy. Somehow she would get Mark to amuse Bobby for
a while so she could start cooking. After she picked up
Sarah in the afternoon everything would be fine. The girl
knew how to keep the other two occupied.

At the *maternelle*, Joan hardly gave Mark time to put
on his coat before she began dragging him down the
street. She was planning her strategy of how to deal with
the *marchant* at the wine store. She had to get him to recommend some good wines without letting him go on forever about temperature and minutes to air and wanting to
know everything on her menu and how she was going to
cook it.

Joan was well past the *clochard* when she tuned into his
refrain, "Des sous. Des sous." It seemed so literary. "Sou"
was a term she knew from reading books in New Zealand,
but had never heard anyone else use in France. Joan cir-
cled an arm around Bobby, opened her bag and shoved
things around inside before pulling up a handful of
change. There were a few 10 franc pieces. She considered

dropping them back in, but thought that giving the old man this much money would make up for past months and make her bag less heavy besides. She took Mark's hand and poured all the coins carefully into his little palm.

She tried to send him on his way toward the *clochard*, but Mark shook his head. It made sense. She was expecting him to give money to someone she routinely described as a smelly old scum. Now, she could hardly expect Mark to trot down there politely and drop the money into the old man's cup. "This is important, Mark. It will make things better." He went slowly at first. But then she could see from his walk that he was proud. She knew he was smiling.

The old man kept singing, "Des sous. Des sous," until Mark was right next to him. The sound of all those heavy pieces falling into the tin cup was like thunder. The *clochard*'s eyes popped open in a dramatic fashion and he grabbed Mark by the shoulders and planted a big kiss on the boy's lips.

Joan started toward them, aware of leaving Bobby behind. The *clochard*'s eyes closed tight and he was kissing Mark hard on the month. Joan began to run. She wanted to yell, but couldn't find the words. A few steps away she stopped, realizing the whole scene was intentional. When she didn't move any closer, the *clochard* opened his eyes and pulled his tongue from Mark's mouth. He looked up at Joan and gave a deep evil laugh.

"Mommy, he had his tongue in my mouth." Mark squeaked as Joan led him away, the *clochard* still laughing behind them.

"No, he didn't, Mark. It just seemed like it."

"He did, Mippy."

By the time Joan reached the apartment door her

breath was short and her chest felt tight. She had been yelling at Mark all the way home. He wouldn't shut up about that man's slimy tongue.

"I'll wash it, Mark, I'll wash it." Joan was trying to get the key in the lock and kicked the door in frustration. She had been wiping her tears as they built up in her eyes. What she really wanted to do was blow her nose.

Inside she pulled Mark by the wrist toward the bathroom. He fell, but she dragged him. "Keep still, Mark," she held him tightly by the back of his head and she pushed his face onto a towel thick with soap.

"It's not me who's dirty, Mip. It's him. Wash him." Mark was struggling to get away and they tripped together on the bath mat. "You hurt me, you fell on me."

"No, I didn't, Mark." When she got up Mark backed away from her. "Come here, Mark. I'm going to make it go away." He stepped back and Joan jumped at him. They fell again.

"You hurt me. You always hurt me." Joan lifted him with one arm around his waist and carried him to the sink. He was wailing so hard she couldn't make out what he was trying to say. Not really caring, she grabbed the bar of soap and put it right into his mouth. He hit her forearm to knock it out, but she pushed the soap between his lips, hitting the bar against his teeth. "Make it go away. Make it go away," she screamed, as though she were speaking to the soap.

Giving up, Joan let Mark slip out of her arm and the soap fell to the floor. She stood in the doorway of the bathroom, Mark wailing on the floor behind her and Bobby was crying. He was still in the stroller. She stared blankly at the baby and leaned her head against the doorframe. Slowly, she mouthed the words, "Make it go away."

After a time, she didn't know how long, the baby's crying got to her. She walked stiffly to the refrigerator and reached in to the top shelf blindly for a bottle of cold milk. At the stroller, she undid the safety strap and helped Bobby slide onto the floor. She kicked the front door shut and dropped the bottle onto the carpet as she walked by on her way to the living room.

Mark and Bobby cried for the longest time, but at some point she realized that everything was silent. She felt an urge to go see what was happening, but was afraid. She didn't want to disturb them. She sat in her chair – tied down somehow. She sat staring at the couch and at the dull light coming through the window. She wasn't thinking anything really, but she knew her lips were moving.

"Joan, where did you get your jeans?" Joan was startled. It was Annette talking to her. Joan didn't expect it. Annette seemed so wrapped up in conversation with Robert and the new guy. Joan wasn't sure anymore if it still was last night, or if it was the morning and she was still dreaming. Annette was sitting close to Robert on the couch. They were both smiling at her. "Don't those jeans look great?" Annette said. "But, then again, Joan would look good in anything, she has such great legs."

Suddenly, there was no one there anymore and Joan was aware of how quiet it was. She shuffled her feet to reassure herself that she was where she thought she was.

"Make what go away, Mippy?"

It was Sarah. With a sudden sense of panic, Joan realized she had completely forgot about going to pick the girl up. Then Joan thought that, of course, she had forgot because she didn't even know what time it was. And this strange logic gave her a sense of relief. "How did you get here?" Joan asked astonished, as if Sarah had come to visit from a foreign country.

"Madame D. brought me."

"I see," Joan answered as though pretending to understand something she really didn't. But the thought of Madame Destroisfleurs brought Joan back to earth and she snapped at Sarah, "What did she say?"

"Is your mother late again?"

Joan was afraid that Sarah might waltz off after giving that smart answer, but the girl seemed to sense her mother's fragility. "Take care of your brothers, will you, Sarah?"

It was dark when Sarah came up beside Joan and stood on her tip toes to look down into the street. "What are you looking at, Mip?"

"Cars."

"Robert's late. But I don't think you'll see the car. Annette wants it."

Joan really didn't want to see her own car. She was looking at the vehicles parked along the street to figure out if Annette really could have been leaning back far enough to have been out of Robert's way or if they had to be kissing. It was hard to tell.

Sarah grabbed her mother's wrist to check the time, "Maybe he drove her home." Sarah's voice sounded strangely sceptical and Joan suddenly feared for her daughter. Joan looked into Sarah's face for any other signs of suspicion. But what she saw was Sarah's horror at her mother's appearance. Joan knew she looked a fright.

When the door opened Joan resolved to put a good face on things. She found a big smile and went into the entrance hall. Her hands were shoved snugly into the front pockets of her jeans and, despite trying to appear relaxed, she couldn't stop herself from curling her body up against the wall like a cat.

"How was your day?" Robert asked, but he didn't seem to notice Joan's appearance or even her cloudy red eyes.

"Joan's had a bad day, Robert." Sarah spoke up from the living room.

Robert looked mildly surprised, as though he was ready to hear all about it, and leaned over and gave Joan a peck on the cheek.

Sarah's voice came out from the living room again, "She needs a real kiss, Dip. You know the kind you're capable of."

A MAN OF STATURE

"A man with a mustache," Martha was thinking to herself, "I always wanted to marry a man with a mustache." She chose a table in the sun, out of the shadow cast by the library.

Stephen was saying: "I would like to have children."

"And you should have children," Martha agreed and added in an encouraging tone, "John Gordon has a daughter, doesn't he?"

"Yes, he does. Do you know John?" Stephen asked.

"No." Martha hoped Stephen wouldn't judge her as someone who pried into other people's business, especially an administrative head like John Gordon, but she really wanted to know more, so she put on her best dry voice, "What's his situation?"

"His . . . his wife . . . how did you hear about John?"

"A mutual friend."

"I see. Well, he was married, his former wife had the child. She's been very supportive. Without her help I don't think he would have made the adjustment to being openly gay."

Stephen, it seemed, didn't particularly want to continue. Martha kept staring.

"She wanted to have a child too. So they have a shared arrangement. He's very close to his daughter."

"I can see he would be a dedicated parent . . . and it is his child?" Martha asked.

"Oh, yes." Stephen opened his mouth to say more

about John, but Martha could see he thought better of it and began to talk about himself: "I would like to have a son."

Martha was exuberant – he was opening up. She held her deadpan expression afraid to speak and give away her euphoria.

"Not that a daughter wouldn't be special too," he added.

Martha flinched when he reached out to reassure her by placing his hand on hers. His hand only made it half way. She hoped she hadn't shown anything in her face.

Stephen went on: "It's just that I think there's something special there – in the father-son relationship."

"Absolutely," Martha agreed.

Martha found out about Stephen by overhearing a conversation he had with her friend Karen.

"Martha, you mean to say you sat behind that partition the entire time listening in?" Karen seemed truly outraged.

"Stephen did all the talking, you didn't say much." Why was Karen so upset. It was not as if she wouldn't have relayed it all word for word anyway. She was so silly sometimes; one of those long and lanky goofy girls, but pretty. Karen was Martha's only real friend around the library. They got together to talk about men and things once a week. Karen was thirty-five, while Martha was only thirty-four. But Karen would have a man when she wanted one – she'd just have to get a little more serious. It just wasn't the same for Martha. She needed to get to know about those eligible quiet men, any way she could. So when she came by to see Karen and heard Stephen in there talking, she just sat down and listened:

". . . I'm happy for having moved up in the administration, don't get me wrong – and I think I should be proud of it – but the hoops you have to jump through. Even something as simple as where you live. I live right downtown, and a lot of the neighbourhoods are not so good, so I don't mention it. Among the staff, they would think it was cool to live on Church Street, but if you're in the second floor administration, you have to live in the right neighbourhood." Stephen paused. "Some things are better not said."

"Oh, for sure," Martha heard Karen say and imagined her shaggy dog hairdo flopping as her head bobbed in agreement.

Stephen continued: "It's sort of expected too that you have children. Now, I'd love to have a son. Actually, I have a real need, you know, as a human being to share my life with a child, with a son."

Martha didn't hear anything from Karen this time, but that wasn't surprising, as far as she knew Karen had no interest in children whatsoever.

"It's finding the right person, that's the problem."

"That's the problem," Karen responded in the same sappy way she did whenever anyone expressed regret.

Martha waited until Stephen stuffed a big fork full of pasta salad into his mouth, then she took a deep breath. "Last month my niece and nephew came and spent the day with me."

"They did? How old are they?" Stephen seemed eager to know.

"Sally is nine and Jeremy is seven."

"You see them often?"

"No, they live in Vancouver." Stephen was waiting to hear more, even anxious for more. Martha was locked by his stare. Finally she said: "My sister was passing through so I took them while she went shopping."

"I see."

Martha was trying not to let her face drop. She should have made more of that. How could she have let it go so flat. Why didn't she talk about the games she had played with Sally and Jeremy.

"I . . . I . . ." Stephen was being polite and filled in the silence. "I really regret that I've waited so long to have children. I'm forty now and I want to have kids while I can still enjoy them. I feel as though it's now or never."

"Yes, that's important." Martha was afraid to say anything, she felt she had blown it already.

"The problem is finding the right person, someone who's willing to put children first and who knows what it means to be in an open situation. Not just that, it would have to be someone compatible, someone with cultural interests, an interesting person. How's your fish?"

"Oh, it's fine. They often do a nice fish here. And yours?"

"Good." Stephen said and they fell into silence.

This was not good, Martha thought. She picked up her knife but it began to rattle against her plate. She was going to try some rice, but was afraid it would scatter all over the table. She had better say something fast she thought, something cultural.

"Not so much now, but I have read a lot of Thomas Mann and Isherwood. Isherwood, I've read almost all of Isherwood."

"Really? What about movies?"

"I don't go to movies much anymore. But videos, I . . . I

28

like videos. I just saw . . ." Stephen was waiting for her to tell him about her latest video, but that was *Mary Poppins*. She had got it just to cheer herself up. She couldn't tell him that. She had seen a couple others last week. What were they?

Stephen came in to rescue things again. "I saw *The Sheltering Sky* a few days back. What a heavy movie, intense. I wouldn't really recommend it."

"It's hard actually for a single woman to get out to movies. Even if you go with a friend, you still end up walking home alone."

Where were things going now? Martha had had such hopes after she overheard Stephen's conversation with Karen. At moments she had even considered her coming attachment to Stephen as *un fait accompli*. Why shouldn't she? She was a bright good-looking woman. It was true that in the past she hadn't given herself as much attention as she should. That would change. She had never gone for the game playing, the flirting, but every girl needed a romance, at least once in her life.

She had a very good jaw line, and cheekbones to complement, and a nice chin, not recessed too far with nothing hanging out beneath, thank God. She could lose a pound or two, but she was still young and carried it well. Her body was good and her hair was dependable. She could wear some heels though. She hated the idea of starting to do that – Karen got away with it. If things went well with Stephen, she'd make the transition. That would put Karen on her guard.

From the moment she tiptoed away from Karen's carrel, Martha had been desperate to talk it over, to chat the whole conversation through again. She'd called Karen up as soon as she got back to her desk to say she had something to discuss and arrange the right lunch spot. But when the appointed day came, she'd left a message: "Sorry, I've got a meeting this afternoon. Call you back later."

When they finally did get together and, of course, after Karen got over her uncharacteristic little outburst over the eavesdropping thing, she did offer some good bits of information. Though, all in all, when Martha considered that Karen had been working in the administration with him for close to three years she realized that Karen didn't know as much as one would expect.

"He certainly seems like a nice man," Martha threw out.

"Oh, he can be. When one of the assistants was sick during her pregnancy he was a gem, let her come in late, let her work at home, but he can be a stickler too."

Martha liked that: someone who knew what the rules were, but who could be compassionate. "He has a lot of responsibility, doesn't he?"

"For sure, and he handles it well."

"I guess he may be next in line for the Chief's job."

"Oh, I'm not sure about that. He's someone who does his job well, but he's just not one of those people who's regarded as driven. You know what I mean; he's got other priorities."

"Family?" Martha asked.

Karen just stared back.

"Brothers and sisters, mother and father, does he talk about them?"

"I've never heard a word about any family."

"Any old girlfriends around the library?"

"Martha," Karen tisked, "I think he's of a different persuasion."

"Oh, I see what you mean." Martha fell silent. She replayed Stephen's conversation and tried to ignore Karen as she talked about that damned stuffy book club. If it was so good why was she always recruiting.

Martha called in sick the next day. Over dry toast she thought about how she would tear Karen's eyes out. How could she have done that, sit there and let her ask all those personal questions about Stephen and not say anything – ask about his girlfriends and then tell her he was gay? How long had she known Karen?

A walk through the Annex had not done much for her anger, but at lunchtime after a glass of white wine on College Street, something struck her. Things were not adding up. Why was Stephen so interested in children? Was he just pretending?

Then she had an idea. When she called Stephen to invite him to lunch, he was downright positive. He even said he knew who she was. It would have been no use beating about the bush, so she had come right out and said it: Karen had told her he was interested in children and so she thought they might have something in common to talk about.

"Karen's a real movie buff." Stephen was trying to help the conversation along. "You must get out with her."

"Occasionally, but Karen and I do dinner more. It's an opportunity for us to talk."

"Yes, that's important, isn't it? To talk things through with a friend. That's something that men don't do enough. That's important for Karen then?" It was an earnest question on Stephen's part, but all Martha could muster as an answer was: "Oh, for sure."

"What does Karen like to talk about?"

"Men," was the answer, but Martha was not about to tell Stephen that. "Books, books and family. She's kind of a home body."

"Really, that's surprising. She seems sort of gregarious for a librarian. Gregarious in a nice way, I mean. Is she from a big family?"

"No, she's an only child."

"What does her father do?"

"He's a retired businessman."

"They get along?"

"Yes, they are very close."

"That nice, that's always nice, isn't it?"

"You work in the CIP Office, don't you?"

"That's right," at last, Martha thought, something I can sound competent about. "The work has been . . ."

"Now, you work with another woman there too – Wendy?"

". . . Wendy," Martha repeated a moment too late.

"She is very good, isn't she?"

"Oh, yes," Martha had to say with some enthusiasm because she was not sure if Stephen meant it or if he was employing the phrase in the more common manner, as a euphemism for "lazy and shameless self-promoter."

"There's just the two of you in the office?"

That's right."

"Let me see if I've got the right person, kind of tall, long hair, athletic."

"Yes, kind of dishevelled," Martha put Stephen on the right track, "usually wears jeans and a t- shirt."

"Yes, that's the one," Stephen laughed. "She's kind of hard to miss, isn't she?"

"Yes, if anyone doesn't know where the CIP office is, I say I work with Wendy."

Wendy was not someone whom Martha would have sought out to confide in, but on the day of her lunch with Stephen she was a little more excited than she realized.

Wendy had blasted in just before ten o'clock. She was particularly antsy, and had barely sat in her chair for five minutes to check for any downloads. That was how they divided up the work; Wendy did all the requests from the large publishers who sent their "cataloguing in publication" information in electronically. Wendy downloaded what they did and occasionally chose one to cause carnage on and show their boss the awful mistake she'd found. Martha handled all the requests from the small publishers who could not do their own cataloguing. Everything had to be checked. In a day she might do six, everyone was different. Whereas Wendy might download one hundred in five seconds. How much verification could she do on twenty-five variations of *Ben and the Fire Engine* verses *Ben Goes to the Fire Station*? It was not exactly the same as assigning a number to *Postmodern Iterations of Five Pre-Victorian Writers, Illustrated, with a Bibliographical Essay and a Forward by Pseudo-Robertson Davies*.

Wendy was pacing back and forth in the little office and digging in her bag for a hairbrush – something was up.

There was a knock. Wendy jumped and opened the door cautiously. "Come in, come in," she whispered.

"Martha, this is Charlie," Wendy was beaming like a teenager.

Martha might have found that Charlie stank if she had dared to get close enough to shake his hand, but as it was she saw that he reeked of attitude. He stood there, one hand on his hip, all six-foot-plus of him, sizing her up and down and up again. A long full mane of hair pretentiously pushed back over his shoulders, he must have prepared

his pose before he knocked on the door. So much manicured aura for someone cloaked in such filth: his jeans,
ripped in strategic places appeared completely composed
of handstitched patches, his t-shirt, still somehow white,
bore testament to an eternity of wear. He carried a sombre sullenness that could never be rubbed out, and yet
when he broke off his lurid stare, his face melted into a
mellow smile that made Martha think, "Here's someone I
could talk to."

"You work here with Wendy?" Charlie asked in a serious way.

"Yes, I do," Martha was suspicious, she knew something was coming. "Why do you ask?"

"Because the two of you are like oil and water. You
know you are very fortunate to work with a woman
like Wendy. She's an amazing woman; she's a fabulous
lay."

Wendy giggled.

"No, I mean it. She's an incredible lay. Not that you're
not. I don't know, I've never slept with you. Really, you
should consider yourself honoured to work with her."

Martha didn't know why she hadn't walked out of the
room, but for some reason she was sitting there, nodding
appreciatively as though they were discussing Wendy's
exemplary work habits. He cast such a spell that she
almost said, "Yes, I do feel honoured."

"You know most women can't handle a compliment
like that."

Again, Martha almost said, "Is that so," but managed
to get a grip on herself.

Wendy took Charlie by the wrist and dragged him over
to her corner of the office. They mumbled a few things
and he kissed her neck. Then she pressed some coins into

his hand, opened the door and tried to sound forceful: "Go down stairs and get yourself a coffee." She laughed and shoved him out.

"By-ye," Charlie said to Martha in a mock drawl.

"Nice shoes," Martha came back.

Charlie looked down. Martha saw him stumble mentally for the first time.

"You been picking through the dumpsters in Rosedale?" Martha was surprised by her own repartee. It was as though she had spoken her thoughts.

"*Rosedale!*" he pointed a finger at her. "Gucci, Gucci," and stepped out.

"Wendy, where did you pick him up?" Martha asked.

"On Spadina, he was busking."

Martha looked like she might suffocate on her own astonishment.

"Don't worry, I made him take a shower first."

Martha stuck her nose back into her terminal and Wendy sat fidgeting and filing her nails.

A few minutes later their boss burst in out of breath. "Wendy, have you got your numbers? How are you, Martha? I have my mangers' weekly in five minutes."

Typical, Martha thought, the entries she had logged were irrelevant.

As soon as the boss had gone Wendy packed up to go. Martha heard her open the door.

Wendy stood there, then offered timidly, "Martha, I'm going to duck out early for lunch, Charlie is . . ."

"Wendy," Martha still did not turn around, "I'm going out for lunch today too."

Wendy approached, "Martha, you're having lunch with a guy?"

"Yes." When Martha turned around she was blushing.

35

"Martha, you've got a date."

"He's a very nice man. Very cultured. Broad interests, aware, you know what I mean. He's very considerate. I've only spoken to him on the phone, but I have seen him around, and I know about him through friends."

Wendy had pulled up a chair. "Yes," she told Martha to go on.

"Well, he's a little older, he has a good job, he's good looking."

"Martha, he's not married, is he?"

"No, no, not at all."

"Okay, what else?"

"He has literary interests; his tastes are similar to mine. I think we'd be a good match."

"Good-looking, good job. Are you sure you've got the whole story?"

"Well . . ."

"Well?" Wendy prompted.

"Wendy, you're not the straightest person in the world. I mean you don't care about all those stupid social conventions. Why should I?"

Martha watched Wendy's shock spread over her face. Martha knew she sounded tongue-tied and a bit like an innocent idiot, but surely Wendy could do a better job of containing her reaction.

"So what's the whole story?" Wendy asked bluntly.

"He's gay, but he wants to have children. I think we could have a good arrangement."

"Oh Martha, don't sell yourself short." Wendy placed her hand softly on Martha's shoulder. "Spruce yourself up a little. You don't have to look that bad. You'll find the right guy, I know you will. Sorry, I've got to go." Wendy got up to go for the door, before she closed it she stuck her head back in and suggested: "Try doing something with your hair."

Wendy was the first topic that had come up at lunch to make Stephen laugh. Martha thought she should exploit this. She had been waiting for something to set the tone of the conversation on a more congenial note so she could take their little talk were she wanted it to go, to bring up the reason for their meeting.

Martha rehearsed a joke to tell about Wendy, but then sighed. What good would belittling Wendy do. Stephen was sitting back in his chair now, looking out over b. p. nichol Lane.

Martha wondered what he thought of her. He was placing his fork and knife side by side on the plate and using both to make a neat channel between his rice and salad. Martha was sitting back in her chair watching him. She hadn't finished her food either. Lunch was clearly over.

Stephen was looking around. At any moment he would say, "Shall we go?"

"You know," Martha had to speak before it was too late, "as we were discussing earlier – about children?"

"Yes," Stephen clued in immediately and smiled.

Martha remained sitting back in her chair and held her head high. She told herself to speak in a clear voice: "I'm not a very conventional person and I'd be willing to set up a situation like that with you. So you could have children."

Stephen's eyes were saucer-wide. Martha could not tell if he was intent on discerning the meaning of her every word, or if he was dumbfounded.

"That's an amazingly generous offer, Martha. I'll have to give that some serious thought."

The next week was exuberantly joyful. Martha knew that things had not gone as well as she had hoped and she was trying to hold on to reality. Stephen and she had not had an immediate personal rapport. That would have to come in time. Stephen was formal and pensive, though considerate. It might take years to build the intimacy she craved, but it would come. It would come through their affinity for culture, their sensitivity to others and, of course, their children.

When the tenth day after their lunch came and Martha hadn't heard from him she began to have doubts. Stephen was such a serious man; he couldn't make a decision like that without really thinking it over. At moments she did tell herself that she should prepare for a disappointment. But she went on making plans, charting out their foreign trips, even decorating the bedroom.

On the Monday of the third week she felt something had to be done. She had been avoiding the second floor but now wondered if she should wander around down there. She kept mulling over what she would say to him if she called. She left work late unable to decide what to do. A few blocks from the library she saw Stephen in the distance crossing at an intersection with Karen. They were holding hands.

Martha went straight home and stood in the bathroom for some time, staring at herself in the mirror. She held her hair in different short styles thinking what it might do for her. Then she took the bottle of pills from the cabinet. She poked her finger in to make sure it was full, then she shook it.

In the living room she sat at the couch and popped the

bottle down on the stack of old *White Bride* magazines she'd bought at a used bookstore on Yonge Street. With the first pill in her hand she started flipping casually through the pages. She stopped at "Canada's Most Eligible Bachelors." The styles were so outdated they made her smile, but the guys were all good looking. Stephen was good looking. Maybe that was it – maybe Stephen was just too good looking. One of the men caught her eye. She held up the magazine and looked at the photo from one angle and then the other. The magazine dropped from her hands and hit the table knocking over the pills. Martha stood there transfixed. Then everything gelled in her mind and she left the apartment heading for Spadina.

It took over a month for Martha to arrange lunch. Karen smelt of a decaying odour. She was sitting up with impeccable posture. She was sparkly-eyed.

"Thanks so much, Martha," Karen finally said after half an hour of this and that, "for bringing Stephen to my attention. There we were working together for years and I hadn't really noticed him. We've seen quite a lot of each other." Then Karen looked into her lap and intoned like a confession: "It's very serous." When she looked up she was beaming like a once envious and now triumphant teenager. "I know this must all sound a little premature, but we have known each other for a long time."

"Karen," Martha said firmly. She appeared calm, but on the inside she was feeling on the verge of hysteria. "Stephen is gay."

They held each other in a stare. Martha pictured them crossing the street. Karen was taller than Stephen.

Finally, Karen threw back her shoulders. "No, he's not."

"Shit, what time is it?" Patrick tried to sit up in bed but fell back down again. The baby was crying. Patrick counted, "One, two," and sat up.

Francesca passed a hand over his back, "Time to go?"

Patrick leaned over and kissed her breast. "Time to go." The two of them jumped out of bed.

Francesca grabbed her housecoat. "You get in the shower. I'll get Nat."

In the kids' room, she picked up the baby who had stopped crying the moment she walked in. "Nathaniel, Sir, how are you this morning? Oh, you're all wet, aren't you?"

Out of the corner of her eye, Francesca saw Sarah, her older child, standing in her crib with an elbow on the railing. Sarah was the family conscience – Francesca was waiting for the zinger.

"Daddy late for work?" came the little sing-song voice.

"Yes, Miss, Daddy late for work. Why don't you get him his cereal?" She swung Sarah out of the crib and the girl ran off.

Francesca came into the kitchen with Nathaniel on her hip. Sarah was trying to hoist the milk pitcher up to the table.

"Oh, damn." Patrick clenched his fist as the milk rolled off the table onto his sock.

"Get a grip." Francesca grabbed Patrick by the lapels of his tweed. "You can have your fag when you get out the door."

Patrick shovelled two big spoonfuls of muesli into his mouth. "Fabulous, Sarah, fabulous, the best."

Sarah looked at the floor and smiled.

At the top of the stairs, Patrick was slipping into his boots.

"Patrick?" Francesca stood beside him. She seemed dejected all of sudden.

"What is it?" Patrick asked.

"Nothing." She ran a hand across his shoulder.

"No, what is it?"

"You said you'd think about Europe."

"We can talk about it at lunch."

Patrick bent over and the three of them lined up for a kiss.

He thumped down the stairs. Francesca and the kids scurried to the front room. They waved as he ran down the street past the school hopping along trying to stuff his blue jeans into his boots, and trying to light a cigarette at the same time.

When he reached work, Patrick had finally calmed down. He walked through the colonnade pulling on a crumpled tie he found in his pocket. When half done up he found a big spot that looked like mayonnaise. He undid it, tied it small end out, then stuffed the offending end into his dark shirt.

He made it past the boss's office and unlocked his door thinking he had made it, but his coffee hadn't even kissed the desk when he heard: "Patrick, problem."

"Oh, damn."

It was Derek. His baby-faced shaved head leaned into the doorway. It went on: "Wieb was down here looking for you. He's on the roof."

"What do you mean 'he's on the roof?'"

"He said there's a matter he'd like you to look into."

"Shit," Patrick showed his teeth.

"Something about a Cabinet Submission, a strategy paper, from PFR."

"I checked into that." Patrick glared at Derek as though that should be the end of the matter.

"He says there's something there."

"Honestly, you'd think the whole world was waiting for Wieb's *Tied-up Loonie* paper." Patrick rubbed his temples, stared at the floor and started off towards Wieb's office. Out in the hallway, he stopped, went back to his desk, reached for the first folder in sight and stooped to slurp the coffee off the lid.

Patrick saw Wieb in the sexy new analyst's office, he was dictating over her shoulder and correcting her spelling as they went. Patrick was going to keep right on moving, but Wieb called out, "How's it going with our response to the PFR paper?"

"Provincial-Federal Relations Strategy," Patrick waved the file folder, "I'm right on it," and he headed downstairs for a cigarette.

Under the colonnade he could hardly hear himself think for all the nesting pigeons screeching over the noise devices meant to keep them away. Who did he know at PFR? Tall, short hair, big eyes, attitude, Joan. That was it: Joan, Joan Carol. He might have to talk to her.

Back upstairs he was flipping through a two-year-old government directory. Derek's head appeared. "Why don't you use the on-line?"

"Stupid thing," Patrick muttered.

"Here, it's easy." Derek went around to Patrick's computer. "What's the name?"

"I need the Manager of Policy at PFR."

A few clicks and a bang later, Derek had found the number. He leaned over to Patrick's phone and dialled. Patrick took the phone and as soon as he heard the voice on the other end he began to turn pale.

"Yes, I understand that we wrote you to say that we did not want to be on the consultation list for the Cabinet Submission," Patrick rolled his eyes. Derek was looking earnest.

"Yes, I do understand that your Deputy has already signed-off based on only minor concerns being expressed, but . . ." she cut him off again. Patrick realized he was getting nowhere. "But could we just see the paper for information purposes? . . . We have certainly sent you Cab Subs at this late juncture . . . Fine . . . Fine." Patrick hung up.

"Get me Joan Carol, same unit."

Derek plugged in the name.

"Joan, Joan . . . No, that restaurant isn't there anymore . . . Yes, we should. Joan, do you think it would be possible to get a copy of your strategy paper? . . . Yes, yes, I understand . . . Just for information purposes, nothing more . . . Why? We've written a paper on tying the loonie to the American dollar . . . Yes . . . the Director, Wieb again . . . How'd he come up with this idea . . . He dug up a statement by the Premier when they were the third party . . . But wait, it gets better. It was in a community paper, a quote from some luncheon talk to the West Orange Rotary. Then he just included it with the usual policy wish list at the beginning of the term. And guess what, they asked for it . . . No, he's not worried about it backfiring. He thinks this is his ticket to the ADM's office . . . Yes, Mary de la Trobe is still ensconced there . . . She's up for factor eighty, and watch she'll take it . . . Of course she's a conservative, but that's got nothing to do with it . . .

She's on her way out . . . She tells them what she thinks . . . You're right, that's a death sentence. Okay, I'll send a fellow called Derek . . . He's to ask for you personally. Joan, thanks a million."

Patrick was in his office pacing in a tight circle when Derek returned. Patrick pulled the stack of dark purple paper from the envelope and asked: "What's Wieb up to?"

"Don't know. He was moving furniture around in the spare office when I passed. Are you doing the communications package?" Derek asked curiously.

"No, Wieb said he was doing it himself. Why do you ask?" Patrick was tilting the pages to catch the reflection off the shiny black ink.

"Can Wieb write? What's with the nifty purple paper?"

"Non-copiable. Find out what he's up to, would you?"

Derek slunk off with an extra wrinkle at the base of his neck.

Patrick fell into his chair and put his boots up on the desk. He checked the *pro forma* to see which ministries had signed-off, then turned to the back of the Cabinet Submission. He was deep into the recommendations when he caught a flash of light off Derek's head. He looked up. The head spoke from the doorway:

"There's some new guy joining the unit, someone with a weird name, Wellington?"

"There aren't any more openings. What new guy?"

Derek shrugged then suddenly looked alarmed and mouthed: "Wieb's coming."

Patrick pulled his feet off the desk.

"Director," Derek mumbled.

"What's the scoop?" Wieb adjusted the jacket resting on his shoulders.

"Not good." Patrick tried to sound neutral despite his words.

"Not good?" Wieb seemed unfazed too.

"It says no new initiatives that might be construed as interfering with federal jurisdiction."

"Did you hear the Rolling Stones are coming to Toronto?" Wieb sang, "Brown Sugar."

"Cool," Derek poked his head back in.

"The reason being . . ." Patrick tried to pull Wieb back down to earth.

Wieb grunted, so Patrick knew he was back on topic.

". . . The centre is planning a new fair treatment campaign, you know . . . and they want to be able to really hit the feds when they cross into our territory . . ."

"And if we're in theirs, we won't have a leg to stand on, so we are not supposed to mess around in their territory. I gotcha," Wieb finished the thought. "That's okay, just give three options in the communications package: a strongly worded statement, a moderate one and a mild one."

"The document does specifically say 'international relations,' and 'monetary policy' are out of bounds." Patrick cringed; he knew he shouldn't have said that.

Behind Wieb's back Derek was mouthing what looked like, "TIM, TIM."

Patrick screwed up his face to show he wasn't getting it. Then Derek drew the shape of the letters with his finger in the air: "C-L-M, C-L-M," for Career Limiting Move."

Wieb was staring at the ceiling, apparently unaware. "The paper actually says that, does it? Well, in that case . . . I heard Jagger on the radio last night. His voice is as good as ever, just as clear as it ever was."

"Really," Patrick tried to look amazed.

"Cool," said the head.

Wieb went straight on: "Use the mild statement for all three options. And the options will be three different media responses addressing why it is appropriate for us to be making a statement on the stability of the American dollar at this time."

"I've got it," Patrick nodded and made a scribble on a sticky pad, then asked, "We've got someone new coming?"

"No one new, Cromwell. His leave is up."

"Really," Patrick swallowed hard, "did you hear from him?"

"He's due back tomorrow and I haven't heard that he's not returning."

Patrick rolled his eyes.

"I've budgeted his salary for the balance of the year," Wieb was insistent.

Patrick figured he knew more than he was letting on.

Wieb turned to leave. "Let's see that communications strategy by two. I'll show it to the ADM at my four o'clock. DMO by five. And make copies of the PFR paper to circulate with it."

Patrick grabbed his pen to take notes again. "By five," he repeated and wrote *"Shit, Cromwell,"* then drew a stick hangman.

Derek took a seat after Wieb had left. "ABM? DBM?" Derek looked confused.

"ADM, DMO. Assistant Deputy Minister, Deputy Minister's Office."

Derek grabbed his clean chin. "Cromwell, isn't he the guy who went off to volunteer in Guatemala or something?"

"Belize. That's the bloke." Patrick held his head in his

hands. The urge was coming on again, the overwhelming urge to call up Lisa and apologize. It had been five years now since Crom had introduced them and they married and split-up in a whirlwind, but still Patrick felt guilty. He squeezed his head and tried to shake himself out of it then stood to go for a cigarette. "Find me a number would you, Derek. A Lisa, Lisa Grimaldi, in Cambridge, Mass. I'll be back in a minute."

Down with the pigeons, Patrick pulled out a cigarette. He didn't smoke when he met Lisa, but he certainly did by the time they broke up.

Lisa was leery of going down the dark stairs into the basement, but it was a church. She was hit by a smell, as though from childhood – the over-waxed linoleum floor. Moving along the hallway, she followed the light from the street-height windows, and then the unmistakable hum of pre-lecture mumbling. It was one of those 1950s wood-panelled recital rooms. Immediately, she caught the eye of the short bug-eyed guy who had told her about the lecture.

He came toward her. "There you are."

Lisa wasn't sure about his smile. What was his name, she wondered. Something strange, something British. He looked a little more smarmy than she remembered. What was it about him? What was off? Maybe his hair. He was the only fellow there with a salon cut. Why had she come?

"Pat. Pat. Patrick," he was calling to someone in the crowd.

Lisa didn't expect to find so many Dr. Martens in a church basement. Her khaki Dockers seemed out of place.

So much black. Now, that was better. Lisa saw a tall fair-haired guy leak out of the crowd.

"Patrick," the smarmy guy said and pointed at Lisa, "this is our new recruit."

Lisa poured on a thick smile for the smarmy guy. He was shorter than she was.

The tall guy said. "Well, Crom, I hope you managed to get a better speaker this time."

That was it, Lisa remembered, Cromwell.

"Great speaker, you know him Patrick, it's Mark. Lisa came just to hear him."

"No matter," the tall guy spoke to Lisa, "I'm sure you could do a better job of choosing speakers. What's your name?"

Crom cut in, "Lisa, Lisa," he had to shout over the feedback from the PA system, "She's American." He poked Patrick in the chest and left for the front of the room.

Patrick motioned to Lisa to take a seat.

A squat looking guy with a long white beard had come to the microphone. Lisa leaned close to Patrick to ask, "Who's the speaker?"

"Mark Carling, a prof from Ryerson." Patrick could smell her hair.

Patrick leaned closer, "You, a student, Lisa?"

"Yes."

From the front of the room Crom was asking everyone to be quiet.

"In Political Science?"

"Yes."

"At York?" Patrick asked.

"Yes."

Tapping on the microphone, Crom asked for quiet again, the room was still humming.

Lisa kept her head down. She stared along the row of Dr. Martens. It seemed they came in two varieties, the bourgeois socialist ones that were so new they smelt of formaldehyde and the others that were boot camp polished. Lisa declined to speculate on whom the latter shod. She looked at Patrick's Docs. They were all scuffed. She looked up at him. His hair was wild. He was cute. She smiled and his eyes lit up. She knew it. He was taken with her big round face – most guys were.

The speaker cleared his throat, said, "Hegel," cleared his throat again and repeated "Hegel," then paused.

Down the row everyone was sitting up dead silent as though it were some sort of invocation rather than an inarticulate academic stumbling.

"This is going to be gruesome," Patrick whispered into her ear. There was a *shush* from behind. "Want to go for coffee?" he asked.

Lisa put an eager hand on his knee.

"Okay, if we're going, we have to go quickly."

Six months after the lecture, Cromwell walked into Patrick's office looking dumbfounded and stared beyond his friend at the life-sized poster of Evita Peron.

"Lisa's father, that's the problem," Patrick offered unsolicited; he knew why Cromwell was there.

"Patrick, what in the world could Lisa's father possibly have to do with it? You've never even met the man." Cromwell rolled up the sleeves of his new plaid shirt.

Patrick rubbed his forehead. "In a sense he has everything to do with it. He's always interfering."

"I know enough about this guy to know he's not the meddling type. You've never complained about him before."

"He's kind of sneaky," Patrick said.

"Why should I lose an entire night's sleep while my wife is sobbing on the phone with your wife."

Crom held Patrick in a stare as though he was waiting for an answer. Crom let out a huge sigh and flopped into a chair. He kept looking at Patrick but then his face fell and he said quietly, "Okay, let's go for a drink. You can tell me about it."

Across the street at the Cock and Bull, Crom peered into the west lounge and caught sight of the Deputy in front of the fireplace. Crom held out his arm to prevent Patrick barging in. The Deputy was seated with two white-haired blue suits, gold chains. They were laughing nervously. Crom said: "We better go upstairs. Patrick didn't like it upstairs – the gaming room had a strong smell of stale beer and the lights flashed obnoxiously.

"A whiskey, please." Cromwell called to the waiter.

"A rye?" he asked.

"A whiskey, a whiskey," Cromwell seemed overly impatient, "a Scotch."

"The same," Patrick said and waited for Cromwell to calm down.

Cromwell bent his head. "I'm sorry, go ahead, tell me the whole story."

"There's not much to tell really. When we got the condo, Hubert said . . ."

"Hubert?"

"Yes, Hubert, Lisa's father."

"Oh, right, Hubert, go on."

"Hubert said that if we bought a condo on five percent down as first-time home buyers that he would pay the five percent. But when his lawyer came for us to sign the papers what I didn't know was that we also signed the deed over to him. When I caught on and told Lisa she already knew all about it."

"What the hell's your problem?" Cromwell said impatiently, "It's like you're paying rent, you didn't make the down payment anyway. I'm sure Hubert knows what he's doing, he's an American businessman, for God's sake."

"This was only supposed to be temporary," Patrick had his story down, "I was going to work for a few more months until Lisa's scholarship money came through, and then we would split the rent."

"Right, right, I remember and then you were to go back and do your PhD."

"The money did come through."

"It did?" Cromwell was genuinely surprised, "I thought you'd been waiting all this time."

"No, it did, but instead of sharing the rent with me she put a wad of it down against the principal on the mortgage. She says that's her contribution."

"She didn't talk to you about it first?"

Patrick shook his head.

"So I see, so I see," Crom said.

"I don't need a luxury condo. We're both going to York, or 'we were' – I had to let my registration lapse."

"Okay, I get it."

Patrick was hoping he had got it all wrong, that Cromwell could have shown him how it all made sense, that he was being overly sensitive. Patrick didn't like the role reversal anyway. When the two of them got together over drinks in the middle of the day, it was usually Patrick giving the pep talk while Crom commiserated on the life of a civil servant.

"What are you going to do, Crom?"

"I've had it with this place. I'm going to El Salvador."

"There's a war on there."

Crom didn't answer.

"Did you do the tax exemption piece Wieb asked you for?"

"No."

"Crom, you've got to do something."

"I know, but I'm not doing it."

"You haven't done a stitch of work in three months."

"I'm going to do something real. This is exploitation, what we're doing here."

"Exploitation, Crom? Wait till you get to El Salvador."

At lunchtime, Patrick took the stairs down to street level. He could see Francesca and the kids across Queen's Park Crescent. They were already spread out with blanket and paraphernalia under the usual tree. He could see Sarah trying to get something out of the big double stroller and saw Francesca jump when it rolled. When she spotted him, Sarah came running and Nathaniel waddled a ways until he fell.

"Tuna or cheese?" Francesca asked.

"One of both," Patrick said cheerfully, but then said nothing. Patrick knew Francesca was thinking about Europe, he couldn't avoid it forever.

"Wieb thinks Crom is coming back tomorrow."

"No, get lost. How come?"

"His leave is up."

"He's not coming back."

"Wieb knows something. He's acting very strange."

"But wouldn't Crom have told you if he was?"

Patrick shrugged.

"Do you think what's her name, Crom's wife, is still friendly with Lisa?"

Patrick shrugged again. The idea that Crom and Harriet were still in touch with Lisa had not occurred to him, but it was possible.

"They were close friends, weren't they?" Francesca asked.

"I suppose so."

Patrick got up to help Nat go around the tree.

"Did you find anything good on Europe?" Patrick asked when he sat back down.

Francesca smiled and pulled a stack of web-page print-offs from her backpack.

When Patrick returned from lunch, he found a sticky on his desk: "*Patrick, L. Grimaldi not in Cambridge, Mass. Directory. I'm on the case. Derek.*" Patrick sat and grabbed a pad of lined paper. He wrote *Com Strat* across the top and stared down the blank page. He looked over to the garbage can. The sexy new analyst walked by running her hand over her bum as she passed by his door. She stopped at the fax machine. Patrick held his pen to write but nothing came to him. He dropped the pen, grabbed Derek's sticky, crumpled it in one hand and threw it into the garbage can.

"You're not practising Max Green."

"Pardon me?" The sexy new analyst was standing in Patrick's doorway. She was wearing a plaid skirt and darted white blouse and held her hands up on the door jambs. Patrick was not sure if *"You're not practising"* was a question or statement of fact. He stared at her trying to figure it out but only became more perplexed.

"The Max Green," she repeated as though Patrick should have known.

"Sorry, I don't follow."

"When I was with the Ministry of the Environment we instituted the Max Green Program. Everyone gets a half litre sized container for their desk top to put all their garbage in. It encourages people to recycle."

Patrick was looking dumbfounded.

"It saves oodles of money."

"Really," Patrick said. "I guess we don't have that program here."

"Yes, you do. This building is on the list."

"I'll have to look for my little garbage can then."

"You do have one."

Patrick smiled and she did an about-face in military style, stood at attention, ran her left hand over her bum, and left.

Patrick ran to the doorway. As she passed by Wieb's office door, her hand, it seemed unconsciously, slid over the round of her bum again. "Bizarre," Patrick muttered, then retrieved Derek's sticky, carefully uncrumpled it and stuck it back onto his desk. He stared at the sticky. It made him think of Lisa. "I'm sorry," he muttered, then shook his head and said aloud, "Get a grip, Patrick."

Could he really talk to her again after all these years? When was the last time they talked?

He rubbed his temples, then ripped the page with *Com Strat* from the pad, rolled it between his hands into a ball and pitched it with some satisfaction into the trash. From the recycling bin, which he kept tucked under his desk, he dug out an old draft of the *Tied-up Loonie* paper and looked for a page with some white space, drew in a box with *Com Strat* at the top and began furiously to write the communications strategy in his tiny scrawl.

When he finally looked up, the sticky was still there.

When was the last time he talked to Lisa? She had called him, a couple weeks after she'd left for the States.

"Were you ever going to call me? I left you a message." It was true, she had. "What have you been doing?" It seemed so strange of her to ask, as though they had spoken yesterday. Patrick had made something up. He hadn't been doing anything but mope and watch TV, but he made up some equally mundane story and for some reason that made him feel better.

"I miss, you. I really thought we were going to be together forever." Patrick seemed perplexed. She had been plotting to go back to the States ever since she got her landed status and unexpectedly ended up with a pile of cash from her foreign student fee refund.

"I might be coming up to Canada, Quebec City actually, for the ARC."

"The ARC?"

"The American Research Council. Yeah, they are going to have their next meeting in PEI."

"Quebec City is in Quebec."

"Oh, is that right, isn't Quebec City that quaint little place with the Anne of Green Gables dolls? Oh, that's PEI, right, right. And when are you going to finish?"

"I'm not going to go back this term."

"No, how come?"

"They told me I'd have to pay for another whole year, because I was off last semester."

"That's outrageous. So you're free and easy for another year."

"I'll try to do some work, but I've got to keep this job with the government to save up my tuition and something to live on."

"I'm still plugging away here."

"Is that right?"

"Yeah, I'm trying to figure out who to work with."

"Uh huh."

"It sure will be tough."

"What, financially?"

"No, at Harvard."

"You got a scholarship then?"

"No, I didn't, but Dad's going to pay for it."

"That's nice."

"Yeah, he made so much money off the condo, it was incredible. It will pay for two years and living and then some."

"Really?"

"Yeah, it was just the right time in the Toronto real estate market."

"Patrick, Patrick, Pat."

Patrick heard his name. He was in a daze. When his eyes cleared, he was amazed to see how much of the Communications Strategy he had written; it ran in diminutive lines down the backs of two pages.

"I found the number."

Patrick looked bewildered.

"Lisa Grimaldi." Derek placed a print-off under Patrick's nose.

Patrick raised his eye brows. "Huh," he looked more closely, *Lisa Grimaldi, Investment Agent, Back Green Investments*. "That's not the one," Patrick said dismissively. Then he noticed that Derek was staring at the crumpled sticky. Patrick ran his hand across it a few times to flatten it a little more.

"I'll keep looking," Derek said.

"Derek, would you mind? We're going to need copies of this PFR paper."

"Sure, how many?"

"Fifteen," Patrick tried to sound apologetic.

"Fifteen?"

"That's standard." Patrick handed over the paper and Derek slumped out. "I've got to type up these notes," Patrick called after him.

Patrick's eyes were jumping back and forth from the clock to the page as he tried to decipher his own handwriting and calculate how many minutes there were before two o'clock.

"Um, Patrick?" The head was back. "How do you make photocopies of unphotocopiable paper?" Derek dangled an ink blackened sheet.

Patrick huffed, "Mother of Mercy. Sorry, it's not you, Derek." He looked at the clock. Then tore off down the hall with Derek on his heels.

Patrick punched the code for the photocopy room door and went straight for a line of keys on the wall. "Key number three," he said and held it in front of Derek's eyeballs. He crossed the room again and counted the filing cabinets, "One, two, three," and put his index finger on the number "three" taped beside the lock. Inside the top drawer he pulled out another ring of keys and flipped through them counting until he got to fourteen. Along the back wall he clicked the door of each cabinet with the key counting to fourteen. He opened it. "Pink paper."

"Pink paper?" Derek repeated.

"Pink paper, dark pink paper in cabinet fourteen. Don't use the light stuff that we use for separators over there on the counter."

Patrick opened a small door at the end of the photocopy machine. "Pink paper in here," he said and pulled the cover sheet off of the dark purple Cabinet Submission, placed it in the feeder bin and pushed "Start." The machine began to squeak and shake. "Damn, I forgot to warm it up when we came in." He walked once around the filing cabinets to cool his heels. When the rumbling stopped he pushed "Start" again. Out came a dirty looking pink sheet.

Derek bent over it, "That's barely legible."

"Ah," Patrick raised his index finger. He removed the pink paper from the by-pass and placed the dirty pink sheet in the feeder. "Lightness," he pressed the button repeatedly. When he pressed start, out came a lightly shaded white sheet, with *Provincial-Federal Relations Strategy* clearly legible.

"Amazing," Derek rubbed his smooth head.

Patrick handed the sheet to Derek.

"Fifteen copies?" Derek asked to make sure.

"Fifteen, and take your time," Patrick answered as he rushed off looking at his watch.

Derek arrived the next morning at the office a few minutes early with his paper and his hot chocolate. He put his feet up on the desk and hoped no one would walk by. It was pretty quiet, since Monday was going to be a holiday and a lot of people were off for an extra-long weekend. He was kind of exposed in his corner carrel, but he didn't hear anything and so opened *The Globe and Mail*. He had just got to the NHL standings when he heard a swish. It was a sound he had heard before, but not for quite some time. It was unmistakable, but what was it doing on this floor – Mary de la Trobe.

Derek sat up tensely, then thought she would be going the other way to Wieb's office – he relaxed.

"Damn," it was getting louder. "Oh, my God." Derek stood up and scrunched the paper shut.

"No, no, don't disturb yourself. May I?"

"Absolutely."

Mary de la Trobe took a seat, the only seat, at the end of Derek's desk. She adjusted her long woolen skirt and carefully tugged on the sleeves of her Victorian blouse. "Your director, I believe, is not in just now." It may have been a question. She stared at Derek until she got an answer.

"No, I heard him say he was going down to HR."

"No. And Patrick?"

"He called this morning. He won't be in today."

"I see. That's good, you're just the man I need to see." She folded her legs and adjusted her skirt again and placed an elbow on Derek's desk.

Derek swallowed. She was tall, she was imposing, she was barely a foot away from him. She was the ADM.

"Now, I had a little read over your monetary paper last night after I saw the Communications Package. I must say, I didn't realize how significant it all was until I could contextualize it in terms of how it would be presented to the public. I think there is just one essential message that isn't getting through in the original paper. Somehow we need to express that while some of the ministry's stakeholders do favour further north-south integration of the industrial sector, most are opposed to increased harmonization in the monetary arena."

"Actually, Ma'am, we did look at that question and we didn't really find that. If you look at the appendix on the review of . . ."

"I think that message needs to be in there. We don't want to mislead the public. Something along the lines of while some of the ministry's stakeholders do favour further north-south integration of the industrial sector, most are opposed to increased harmonization in the monetary arena."

"We did thoroughly research that issue and that is really not the case."

Mary de la Trobe looked away and took a shallow, but audible, breath. "A line such as while some of the ministry's stakeholders do favour further north-south integration of the industrial sector, most are opposed to increased harmonization in the monetary arena."

Derek suddenly felt nauseous. He reached for his copy of the *Tied-up Loonie* paper, which he had revised so many times he knew by heart, and quickly thumbed to the commentary on stakeholder positions. "There are two places were I think it could go. Here in the body of the paper under Stakeholder Concerns or up front in the Executive Summary."

Mary de la Trobe was looking stony faced.

"Or both perhaps?" Derek offered.

"In the body of the paper. I think that will be fine."

Patrick rolled over in bed. He didn't hear anything, but something must have woken him up. It had to be Nat. He might play in his crib for a minute. He rolled back and put an arm around Francesca and whispered into her ear, "Am I late yet?"

Francesca brushed his hair back and held his face in her hands. "Oh, you don't look well."

"I don't feel well. I think I'm going to be sick today."

"Great," Francesca said, jumping up in bed. "I'll send the kids down the street to Mary and Martha and we'll go for brunch."

At the restaurant, Patrick steamed his head over a bowl

of *café au lait*. He was waiting for his eggs benedict; anything to make him feel like it was the weekend. He and Francesca were a little stumped for words. Most of their conversation together centred around organizing the kids. They didn't have much practice in conversing on things they wanted to talk about. Patrick couldn't stop thinking about work, which was obvious to Francesca, though she was polite enough not to bring it up. Europe was circling somewhere in the air.

"Feeling guilty?" Francesca asked.

Patrick nodded.

"Why don't you go give a call? The eggs benedict will take forever anyway."

Down the corridor, the payphone handle was greasy and there was clanging and cursing from the kitchen. "Derek, what's happing?"

"What's happening? Everything happened, Patrick, everything."

"What do you mean 'everything happened'? It's only ten-thirty. Did Cromwell come in?"

"Yes, Cromwell came in. He's a funny guy, you know. Mary de la Trobe came down . . ."

"But what about Cromwell?"

"Yes, Crom was here, but I better tell you about the ADM first. She came down when Wieb was gone and demanded I change the paper, like completely."

"And what did you say?"

"I said I would."

"I know you said you would, Derek, but what did you tell her you would change?"

"It doesn't matter now, because when I told Wieb, he said the Deputy had changed his mind."

"Changed his mind?"

"Yes, the paper isn't going anywhere. It's dead."

"Did he say why? Forget it. I know why. And what's Crom doing?"

"Crom, what a neat guy. He came in and said he was reporting for work. So Wieb took him down to his office. They chatted a bit, Crom said he was interested in the voluntary exit package. Then Wieb said he should talk to HR so he took him down there. Crom asked for a form, the HR Director filled it out, Crom signed and they gave him a cheque for six months wages. He stayed around long enough to show us some pictures though. What an amazing place he's got. It's a huge house with a ten foot fence around it and guard dogs. He had pictures of his office in town. He says he has thirty employees. Some sort of computer consulting firm."

"Is that right? I never would have guessed," Patrick said. "I've got to go, my eggs should be here now."

"Wait, I think I found something for you, your Lisa number. It's . . ."

Patrick heard a ding form Derek's computer.

"What's this?" Derek said, "An announcement from the Deputy. *Retirement*."

Patrick thought about his egg yokes congealing while Derek read.

"Mary de la Trobe is retiring and guess who is going to be acting ADM?"

"Wieb."

"You got it. But you'll never get this one. Guess who is acting for him?"

Patrick didn't say anything.

"The SNA."

"The SNA," Patrick sounded angry. "Who's the SNA?"

"The Sexy New Analyst."

The receiver slid off Patrick's shoulder. When he got it back onto his ear, Derek was asking, "What's her name again?" But he went on, "Oh, yeah, I think I've found your number. 'Lisa Grimaldi,' in the Harvard Grad. Student Directory."

"No," Patrick said, "that's not the one. No, that's not her. Thanks for trying though."

Back at his table, the waiter had just dropped off two plates of eggs benedict. Francesca was smiling. "Is Crom back? she asked.

"No, he's gone for good. Where in Europe are we going?"

IN THE TIME OF TALKING

At lunch, Grandmother wasn't talking. She kept her hands busy with her soup while she stared at Grandfather and me across the little table. The three of us ate almost the whole meal before anyone said anything. Finally, Grandmother gave in and muttered something about whether Betty would be coming over in the afternoon tomorrow instead of the morning as usual.

Then Grandfather said, "Those rodents are around again," trying to cover-up for the gun shots. "They'll be eating up the garden," he added in a matter of fact way.

Grandmother stared him down with a truly filthy expression. But the really amazing thing was that Grandfather turned to me and said: "Isn't that right, Jenny?" as if I could have answered.

Grandmother let it pass at that. For all her cruel judgements, she was a forgiving person. Though had she known about the dead doe in the forest behind her home, I doubt the gun would have been around much longer.

Until I saw the court documents, Philip, I always thought you knew my grandparents. That was the same time I met you, the summer I spent with them. I can't really remember first meeting you. I've a vague recollection of the social worker who came to pick me up and take me into the city for my appointments. You'd watch from the observation room, while the worker tried to play with me and get me to interact. You'd come in at the end and make a few suggestions. When you left you would crouch down and say: "It's good to see you, Jenny." You had that pretentious goatee even then with the points cutting up into your cheeks. I remember your white coat. And the toys were for kids.

All those years ago, I sat in my grandparents dusty living room staring at the floor and visualizing my mother through the rear window of her car as she drove away. I saw myself, as I still can, standing perfectly still at the edge of the driveway watching the car disappear down the dirt road. I watched until the last small cloud of dust flattened into the distance.

"Pull up your socks, girl. Girl. Girl."

I pretended not to hear. It was no good – Grandmother knew I could understand.

She sat on the couch beside her friend, Betty, a fat lady who wore heavy brown stocking rolled into a coil above the knee. I was made to sit on the stool in front of them. Grandfather sat in his chair, never saying a word and looking away as if his mind should not be pestered with women's talk. He was a cold man.

I hid on the stool as best I could, slouching over my legs.

"She used to talk." Grandmother had a drawn voice. "Yes, she used to, but she doesn't say 'boo' to anyone now." Grandmother's jaw dragged.

Betty repeated, "She doesn't say 'boo' to anyone now," in the same tone and the two of them nodded.

I dug my chin deeper into my knee.

Grandmother tisked.

With her eyes bearing down on my head she spoke into the silence, "She'll be saved because she's innocent. That's God's way of blessing those who are dumb."

I understood what she meant perfectly well. I felt ashamed. Betty was looking at me with a screwed-up smile. I stared back with hate. I could feel it. There was hate between us. Why should Betty hate me? It seemed as though she was taking advantage of a free chance to hate – a chance to hate without any consequences. Perhaps she got pity and hate confused. I did hate her back, I must admit, Philip. She was a dumpy person. But I think I could have tolerated her had she done the same for me.

I certainly thought twice when Sally called to ask me to take part in the study. I felt resentful, thinking it was terribly insensitive of you to have someone call up after two years to ask me to dredge up all that crap, especially when you knew I wanted to leave it behind. Then I began to feel there was something unresolved between us and I wanted to see you again. So by the end of the telephone conversation, I was saying I would come.

As I could have predicted, everyone was new at your office. Sally was not what I expected though – she had a warm side. It was so funny when she told me what she did. "You're a social worker? I asked.

"I'm the interviewer," she answered flatly.

"Yes, I know you're going to interview me, but are you a psychologist, like Dr. Armin?"

"No," she laughed and put a hand on my shoulder. "Philip is a psychiatrist. I'm an interviewer; that's my job."

It hit me so hard to see you, Philip, I knew you would arrange a meeting somehow. I felt bashful when you walked in on us – your deep caramel voice always abrupt: "Hello, Jenny," and the look that was clearly an interrogation but hovered at the edge of a smile. I had to speak and I told you I'd gone back to school even though I'd promised myself I wouldn't tell. I suppose that was your job, Philip, getting people to talk.

When I was leaving you emerged again. Out of the blue, you asked if I wanted a summer job. "Nothing too exciting, filing and stuff for the study." I was thrilled, shocked but thrilled. You didn't wait for an answer, you just said, "Well, then, let me introduce you to my doctoral student. She's in charge of the study." So you took me to see Ann. My first thought was "she's cute," and "what hair," and I remembered the string of assistants you had over the years.

It was from something Ann said that I first figured out how I fit into your little world. A few days after I began working, I went to her and poured on my meekest voice, "Ann, Ann." I couldn't get her attention; she was concentrating so hard. "Ann, what does Dr. Armin study?" I had to ask a second time. Finally, without stopping writing, she said, "*We* study a lot of things, but mostly chemicals in the parts of the brain that effect speech."

That was the moment things began to fall into place – I was a speech problem. I was not your patient, and you were not my counsellor.

The sitting room was a stuffy one, especially with Grandfather in his chair. It had small carpets thrown down like patchwork, rich with dust. The only furnishings were Grandfather's chair, the couch, the stool I was relegated to and an old upright piano. The piano was never played, so I couldn't understand why a music book stayed open on it. Yet I'm glad that music was there. It gave me a sense of something more in the world – of things I was cut off from in my grandparents' cottage. I'm sure the piano would have meant more to me if Grandmother had not covered it with porcelain knicknacks. Any space that could be found in the room had something of the sort and they all had lace doilies.

At eleven the cuckoo clock wound up and Grandmother watched the chains move. After the bird had made his appearance she said, "It's eleven o'clock." This was the sign that it would soon be time for Betty to leave. Five minutes later the pendulum clock sounded. Then Betty adjusted the cushions behind her and wobbled awkwardly on the couch, because only her toes touched the floor.

"Elli-Sue has had her third abortion," Betty said to aggravate Grandmother.

"We have never been so blessed as since the day we banned the television from our home," Grandmother said to prevent Betty from telling what her friends on the soaps were doing.

I remember Grandmother blaming the television for being the cause of my not talking.

"Television is at the bottom of more problems than just dumbness. Drugs and violence too are getting worse and worse."

Betty and Grandfather could have no reaction to this. What could drugs and violence have to do with them out in the middle of nowhere?

"I tell you this world is gun crazy and all because of television. There isn't a day that passes without someone being shot. There'll be no guns in the Next and He would like it to be the same here." Grandmother talked on when she sensed no one was listening. "Dad is very particular with his gun. That's why he keeps it in the shed. If we did not live out here, there would be no gun at all."

The idea of a gun impressed me. I wanted to see it and imagined it might look like a heavy army rifle. I must have gaped wide-eyed at Grandmother, because I always did when something struck me. How could I not know it with her forever telling me to close my mouth.

You must have got much the same reaction from me, Philip, as did talk-of-the-gun, when you dropped your line about my going to the conference. You were having a boast with Ann and Sally – how Ann was going to give the paper: how Sally was going to man the poster; and you, you were going to deliver the plenary session; and how the research community was counting on you to do it right; because high ranking government officials were going to be there and you needed to hit them up.

I was sitting off to the side and you turned to me with a rare smile: "Why don't you come to the conference? You did all the work." Finally, you were acknowledging my effort, at least that's what I thought you were doing – I'd waited so long. In my own little way, I was honoured.

At the reception after your talk, you popped over for a confidential word with Ann and Sally so everyone would know we were "with you." Sally had me decked-out in a tight low-cut chiffon thing. She could have played Scarlet in what she was wearing. All through the reception, I stuck to her like glue and thought about how I wanted to have her dress. Ann was trying to keep her distance from us, but I guess you had a different idea when you whispered into my ear: "Why don't you ask Ann what time she would like to go." As if it mattered. I had to work my way through the crowd and then wait for her to acknowledge me. She was screwing up her forehead like she always did when talking to anyone she didn't know, as if she had to prove she could concentrate even though she was gorgeous.

When the bureaucrats left, the buzz in the room filled with talk about your speech. Your colleagues came one by one to pat you on the back. You had hit on just the right mix of jargon and "recent discoveries" of linkages between behaviours and identifiable parts of the brain. Your slides were gruesome, but the audience got the point. All the typical frontal lobe injuries and what the research of you and your colleagues was going to do for these unfortunate victims.

As the room thinned, Ann couldn't get away from us anymore. Lined up behind you we tried to look studious, but were seen for what we were: we looked like the three graces.

I heard you turn down several invites to dinner. Then the four of us left.

"You were a hit, a real hit." Sally jumped up to kiss you on the cheek.

Ann had to get her five cents in, "You know, Philip, I think your speech is going to have a big impact."

Feeling the excitement I wanted to say something too and I chirped like the little bird I was: "It was great." You came back with a smile, "You think so, Jenny?" said like it mattered to you. "I even understood some of it." You laughed and wrapped an arm around my shoulder, then pulled me tight; years of resentment slipped away. Laughing, we packed into your Beemer. Sometimes understanding comes very late to us – as it was for me. It was not until we were driving to Jordan for dinner that I clued in. I was in the rear seat with Ann. As we drove through the country, I watched the back of your head like I watched mother's when she drove away leaving me with my

70

grandparents. It was an epiphany, the realization that there was a connection between you and my mother's departure.

Despite all that, or maybe even because of it, you loomed large in the great cavern of everything I thought I had missed in life. Funnily, I thought you were actually trying to make up for all those years of callousness on that trip to Jordan. I'd never seen you so verbose and you were such a gentleman giving me your arm as we walked through the village. True, you were riding high on your success at the conference. The restaurant was the poshest place I'd ever been and the *maître'd* the first man who ever held my chair. A fact that was lost on you, but certainly not on Sally or Ann.

While the twilight lasted, the view of the valley was magnificent from our table. Sometime in the not too distant past, it had been a good place for hunting.

The forest behind my grandparents' cottage offered me a whole new world, a world inhabited, but not by people. It must have been on the second day I was there that I ventured out beyond the few small hills at the end of my grandparents' yard and discovered the stream. I remember how eager I was to follow it and I did trace the stream a long way. Had the ground been flat, I would have been far out of sight of the cottage. Still, I couldn't explain why everything was so different. Odd things were all around me: giant ferns and big round trees that seemed young. The ground was a soggy bed of deep green moss.

When a branch came loose in the stream, I thought for sure someone had moved it. No one was there, but I stayed still anyway and waited. After I felt safe again, I took a few more steps. Straight ahead of me, I became aware of a sound. I had been hearing it all along, but only when I could see the water falling did I realize. It was beautiful, Philip. If you could have seen it, as I first saw it, then I wouldn't have to explain so much. I know its beauty now as I knew it when I first saw the falls. Just then it looked frightful. I'd return if I could be sure it would be the same. Though at that moment, I felt I had to flee.

You think I'm silly, don't you, Philip, for wanting it to be the same? You probably think I ought to go back and see how it's different and that I'd grow from the experience. I couldn't. The falls are too important, Philip.

I had the feeling the falls belonged to someone, I suppose I've never completely lost it. Someone owned the falls and didn't want me to see them, they wished to keep them a secret. I remember backing away. Suddenly, I was afraid I had wandered too far. I backed up until the falls could not see me and retraced my steps back to the cottage.

"Oh, this is so difficult." Sally flopped her head and rifled through the pages of an interview she was working on. "This is frustrating," she shrieked for effect.

She kept moaning until finally I said, "What is it, Sally?"

Ann had caught her discussing one of the files with a friend on the phone and said the study would be ruined if Sally wasn't completely impartial. I didn't want to talk to Sally about it; she wouldn't stop.

"I was just going over your file."

She knew I'd hate her for this. She did it anyway.

"I can't seem to fit you into a category. The questions

from your interview suggest you were a 'childhood autism,' 'stereotyped ritual, strange behaviour.' The files from your therapy don't show anything like that. There's no report of a psychiatric disturbance, so that would suggest to me 'childhood schizophrenia.' Oh, what to do?"

"Sally, what are you doing with the files from my therapy?"

"Oh, I have everyone's."

"Those files are confidential. You can't use them for this."

Sally held up the form I had signed that first day I came in.

I sat there shaking, shaking in a cold sweat. I couldn't look at her after that.

The next day, I was in the coffee room at lunchtime. She came in and before I could do anything to avoid her, she grabbed me by the wrist. "Let's go shopping." That's when she bought me the dress.

I thought it was just the dress when I caught you staring at me over the wine list. After you ordered a bottle, you excused yourself and Sally followed on your heels. Ann was studying the menu like it was some sort of cipher. In the hallway, I watched Sally slip in front of you. You gave her bum a discreet little squeeze and she stretched her neck back for a kiss, but you had turned to wave to a man I'd seen at the conference. I lifted the cover of the menu for a quick peek and decided maybe I'd just ask for a Caesar salad.

When you returned, Sally flopped herself down with a whimper of satisfaction. Ann rolled her eyes and took your hand underneath the table. You looked at me. "Jenny, may I order for you?"

"I'd be delighted." That line, at least, I knew.

When my neck reached over the bank, I gave a quick look into the forest. It was the same in every direction. If I went in, I might get lost. Out of fear, I looked back at the falls. I knew I must keep a sense of where the falls were.

Sunlight reached into the forest, so it never had a dark, scary feeling. Still you couldn't see very far. Even when I climbed up and stood on the edge of the bank, the plants were too dense. Most of the forest was old tall trees, though at my line of vision, it was all dead limbs, saplings, giant ferns. As I made my way in, I had to go around and over things because the ground was uneven. The fear that something was always beyond what I could see made me peer around whatever was before me. With every noise I made, I hesitated. Might I disturb someone? With every step farther into the forest and away from the stream, I was more afraid a reproach would come from somewhere.

No wonder when I saw the clearing, I panicked. I turned back to where I thought the falls were. The forest was all around me. The only landmark I had left was this open space. I went toward it. I don't know why. I was afraid of it. Not of it really, of what might live there. Yes, I had been seen, Philip. Someone was around there and had been watching me all along. I stayed low and looked carefully into the clearing. It was an almost round space as big as the cottage. After I searched a bit, I wasn't sure if it was a person. I couldn't see anything. Someone was there.

I wound to the right. The sun was coming in from that angle. Feeling a certain boldness rise up in me, I worked my way right up to the edge. There, I began circling the clearing just outside the line of trees that formed it. When I reached the spot, I knew that was it. It was like an entrance. I stood there a moment then stepped in.

As soon as the sun hit me, I had to sink down into the grass. It started coming at me from all sides. I began twirling around on my hands and feet on the ground and looking frantically in every direction to see where it was coming from. I rolled into the middle with my body mangled on the ground. From there, I watched the edge of the clearing to see whoever or whatever might come in.

It didn't want me there, though it would tolerate me. There was nothing I could do to harm it.

What would you have done, Philip? There was no denying it. I knew that whoever it was, was there. It left me to myself, as I was sure it would. Yet, I only could have gotten to where I was by challenging it. Yes, I had challenged it, Philip. I had forced it to recognize me.

It is strange to me that you had seen and spoken with my mother after I had known her. How I've wondered exactly what transpired between you the last time you met. I've imagined every possible word, every congenial twist of hers lips, every flash of misgiving she might have had. I know every mole on her face, every hair of her widow's peak.

That was the enigma, wasn't it, Philip? How could I have remembered her so well and not known a thing about the time we were together?

"Close your eyes. Think about your mother. Tell me about her."

"She's smiling. She seems happy. It's a happy moment.

She's trying, she's trying to be happy. She's saying my name."

"Where are you?"

"Fuck you, I've told you I don't know. How many times have I told you I don't know where I am. I don't know who else is there."

"Can you remember a time when she wasn't trying?"

"No, no, I can't, but she wasn't always trying because of me."

"When she wasn't trying because of you, did you speak to her?"

"Yes."

"About what?"

"I don't know. All I know is that it was in the time of talking."

That has been the tie between us all these years: you trying to use my mother to get to the episode that precipitated the departure of my speech, and I desperately hoping that you would reveal something of her to me.

You were so disappointed, hurt, when I said I wasn't going to come for my appointments anymore. You thought you were on the verge of something. Getting something to come out. You thought I was afraid of it, afraid of the truth you would bring out and that was why I was quitting. That's how you tried to make me feel anyway.

I'm not sure you were on the verge of anything. Maybe we have to think we're on the verge of something.

"Well, Jenny, you know I'll miss our meetings." You were wounded and what a drop of defences. It was so uncharacteristic. I thought it was a ploy.

I knew I was leaving something undone. I didn't see the point. I was fed-up with your constant picking. I was talking. I was functioning. I was learning again. What good was going to come from endlessly digging up the past. Sometimes you have to accept your pain and move on. It's a simple concept I don't have to explain to you. Maybe you thought I wasn't there yet.

"Yes," said Ann like a child when three flamboyant parfait glasses of chocolate mousse mysteriously arrived. I was watching your image begin to take form in the big windows overlooking the valley as the evening light came on. Looking at you there, looking at me, in those few moments after the main course had been cleared, I knew you never would have been able to look at me in an admiring way, if I had not, by leaving therapy, put that tiny step of distance between us.

Sally asked if you wanted her dessert. When you refused, she sent it back. That didn't stop her nibbling away at mine. Ann was devouring hers, annoyingly scraping the glass. When finished, she let the spoon drop with a clink and then started openly stroking your hand on the table. I guess you didn't give a damn.

"May I?" you said reaching out for a taste of my dessert.

Ann stuck her hand out to prevent you. "You could have had some of mine."

You ordered a second cognac. You were staring openly at me then.

I laid on one of the hills beyond my grandparents' cottage like a spy. Nothing was going on. Nothing ever went on. It was such a dead house. Of course the shed was there. The shed with the gun. It was just one hundred or so feet away. An old shed of unpainted boards was a poor home for a gun I thought.

No one was watching. Why shouldn't I go and see it? Nothing was stopping me. I stood up and walked straight over to the shed. Before I dared go in, I looked defiantly at the cottage. The kitchen window was dark. So I lifted the wooden latch.

No gun, just some gardening tools and a clutter of rusty things. Then I spotted it above my head. It was an old, small rifle hanging from a beam on two nails. I was shocked. I really was expecting something big in a glass case. I stepped back to stare up at it. A step too many, I suppose, because my shoulder was grabbed. I knew it was Grandfather. I was afraid of him. Not that I thought he would hurt me – I just knew I'd be better off if I avoided him.

"So you like my gun." He had a smile I didn't trust and he was excited in a way I never imagined he could be. I think he was expecting me to answer him, but I just gawked. "Want to see it?" He had a childlike way, perching, and supporting himself with his hands on his knees.

"Stand back," he said. When he stood straight the rifle was just above his head. His arms brought it down stiffly as though he had arthritis. He put it up to his cheek, put on a deadly earnest expression, and aimed it at me.

I was terrified. After a moment, I cringed. He was waiting for that. Then he let out a big chuckle and let the gun down holding it in one hand by the barrel. He kept laughing smugly to himself and took some bullets from a box in a drawer of his workbench.

"Come on," he said and reached out to take me by the wrist. I don't remember if I shied away or if he didn't care to reach far enough, but he missed. I wish I could remember, Philip.

Behind the shed, Grandfather pointed the gun at a tree off his property. He kept adjusting his aim and replanting his feet. When it went off, I was watching the tree. I heard the crack and saw the bark shatter in every direction. I was still tense from the shock when Grandfather reloaded. He turned toward the cottage, then shot again. I was impressed. Over and over again, I heard the crack of the gun and saw the bark fly.

Ann came running in one morning with her hands over her face. She went straight for her office and closed the door. Sally took a few steps after her and leaned an ear to listen. When the sobbing started she went in. I couldn't make out what they were saying, Ann was crying so much. I heard Sally's, "Oh, Ann, oh, Ann." She was probably draped over Ann's tear-soaked mass of poofed-up hair.

You came in a minute later with an armful of files which you smashed on Sally's desk. Then Ann opened and slammed her door. You didn't look at her. You didn't look at me. You just said, "I'll be next door at the Clarke," and left. All was silent for some time.

When I came back from lunch Ann was waiting for me. She shoved an envelope in my face. "Give this to Dr. Armin. It's very urgent. That means he needs to get it now." No "Under the circumstances," no "Would you mind, Jenny?" Nothing. She just turned her back on me and returned to her little cave.

We hadn't heard from you all morning. I thought I could get the receptionist at the Clarke to do the dirty deed, so I went over and walked up to the second floor lobby – what a lump in the throat that was. How many times had I waited the proverbial extra ten minutes out there on one of the tired vinyl chairs while you ushered clients out the other door. The receptionist wasn't around. I checked the book – no appointment. I thought maybe I'd just leave the envelope on your chair. My hand was stretched out to the doorknob, when I suddenly thought, maybe he's napping. I turned it gently.

You were screwing Sally on your desk with your back to me. She was naked, her legs wrapped around you. She still had her sandals on.

The room had the same old smell, the same busy voodoo carpet. There were a few new clay totems, each with its own undefiled spot from which to survey things. You'd added a large African mask over your chair – the kind that comes from a psychiatrist's supply catalogue – with real matted hair.

Sally opened her eyes and closed them slowly with a smile of recognition. Her mouth opened like yours, sound was trying to escape, necks were stretched, but there was only the quiet bumping of flesh.

I backed out as I had come in and pulled the door silently. A few steps away, I saw I was still holding the envelope, so I turned and crouched and shoved it under the door with purpose. I listened to it skid across the carpet.

As we left the restaurant, Ann was sticking close to you. We shuffled toward the front door. The waiters were smiling – we had stayed late. One held my hand at the step up to the foyer. The *maître'd* signalled to you with the slightest twist of his head. You leaned his way. "Are you driving, Sir?" His eye brows rose in great arcs. You shook your head smugly. He was already pulling a bottle of cognac and a miniature snifter from beneath the reservation table. He filled the glass to the brim. Sally stepped in to smell the contents. You took the glass but hesitated – I thought you might balk. The *maître'd* said: "*Santé.*" Sally put a hand on your back, as if to give it a pat when you coughed. Ann was jockeying for position with no place to go. You downed the glass. Your eyes popped – a divine smile.

I took a last look at the valley. The light had faded and the greens had turned deep dark, decomposing greens, into the heart of the valley.

What could have made such a noise? It was not the falls. It came from the opposite direction. Somehow I knew I had to find out. I was too afraid to move. I would rather have slowly turned about and crept away. How could I stay in the clearing and leave whatever it was free in the forest? At least, I had to identify it.

I stood and went toward the spot where I had heard the noise come from. It didn't matter how much noise I made. If the thing hadn't fled when it heard me, it would stay there for reasons of its own. I really was scared, Philip, but I knew it had to be done.

I didn't know what to think when I saw the fawn standing there awkwardly and trembling beside the carcass of its mother. I know I was relieved to find I didn't have to be afraid anymore. I suppose that's not the sort of reaction you're looking for. Is it, Philip?

For a moment, I stared at the doe, the dried pool of blood. It impressed me to think something so large could be dead. When I looked to the fawn, it was looking back at me, right into my eyes. Why? Why look at me? Why bother? I looked away and started walking back to the falls. All the way back, I kept my arms and shoulders stiff.

There you go thinking me cold-hearted again, Philip.

You could probably analyse everything you know about me in terms of my walking out instead of facing up to things. Don't worry, the story isn't over yet, I hadn't forgotten the fawn. I've never forgotten it.

When I turned sixteen some old tawdry clerk from Children's Aid had me come in to fill out a plethora of forms to release myself to myself. There was an exhilaration in finally ending the shuffle of place to place, worker to worker, but the event was not without its melancholy.

"This is for the trial documents."

"What do you mean?" I asked.

"To turn the documents over to the Children's Aid."

"Well, can I see them?" I was polite.

She put her hand on my wrist: "You don't want to see them, Dearie."

I stared.

She kicked her chair back with an awful rasping noise.

A discussion went on in the next room for some time. Finally, I heard a raised voice: "If she's that stupid, give them to her." A few signatures later, I was out on the sidewalk with three filing boxes.

Great wads of blackout made it difficult to piece together the story, but it started to make sense when I found Betty's affidavit – it could only have been Betty's. Strange to think such a little toad like that could have destroyed a family – family such as it was – me and my grandparents. "The child is not cared for." "She spends her day in the forest." "She goes without meals." All along I thought my grandparents had given up on me too.

We all jostled together in the night air on the stairs leaving the restaurant. Ann and Sally were holding you, afraid you would trip – you had an arm around both their waists. I walked ahead listening to the stones on the path and the giggles of Sally and Ann mingling together. You ran ahead to catch me, I suppose to show you could still walk straight. With an arm around my neck you pointed out a constellation I'd never heard of. It was a night to make me feel like a bit player, but when you dangled the car keys in front of me, I felt triumphant.

I watched Grandfather wander toward the cottage. In my zeal, I saw him turn half an eye toward the spot on the hill where I was hiding. He puttered around on the veranda doing exactly what, I don't know, but not staying still – that's for sure. When he went in, I felt I had won and that I could finally make my assault on the shed. Never did I think Grandfather wouldn't be watching from inside. All I needed to do, though, was to get an old rope off the outside wall and he would have to be looking at the right spot just when I passed to catch me. To confuse him, I moved about behind the hill so he wouldn't know quite where I was. Then I ran for the rope, lifted it off its nail and was on my way.

Deep in the forest again, I tried to pick up my old trail, but that wasn't easy. I was afraid of being stuck there all night. Now and again, I found what I thought had been my path, only to lose it again. I was searching for the fawn, Philip, and I had the rope with me. Yet, even at that point, I really didn't know what I was going to do.

When I did come across the fawn, it was the same as when I had left it – shaking terribly and tittering as though it might fall at any moment.

When I crept close, I thought it would jump about and

maybe bite me. It couldn't even react, Philip. Not even to defend itself could it have broken out of that awful shaking trance. It didn't move or turn its head when I put my hand on its neck. That was one of the most disturbing sensations I've ever felt. As I moved my hand over it, the tremors from its body passed into mine. Its short fur was sweaty and cold and I could feel all of its bones.

I would have to take it away from there. Where was I to take it? Nowhere near the cottage. The clearing at once seemed to be the right spot. Would the creature let it stay there? Maybe if it was me who brought it in the creature would let it stay. I had to give it a try, Philip.

Before I put the rope around the fawn's neck, I thought of how I would have to be gentle. I knew it would struggle and it wouldn't be used to having anything on it. I thought, too, that it might run away, but if it did, it wouldn't go far. It couldn't leave its mother, though she wasn't much use to it. When I bent over to put the rope on, its eyes didn't follow me as I expected. I thought everything would be easy then – I even thought it liked me until I tried to pull it away. For such a weak, shaky looking animal it held its ground. I pulled hard, but couldn't move it and whenever I let up, it would turn its head back to its dead mother. There was nothing to do but pull harder. When I put all my weight on the rope, its knees gave in. I felt the pain myself when I heard the fawn's knees drag across the ground. I thought that was it, but after struggling on its own and bobbing its neck it got up again.

Ann and Sally were put out when they got to the car and found me in the driver's seat. I thought at first you were turned toward me to watch how I drove, but through a few awkward turns I realized you couldn't give a damn about your car, it was me you were looking at.

After a while, Ann and Sally came to life again. They were cuddling and singing songs. You were staring into my lap. I looked at you – you looked in a haze – and I thought, "Yes, I want this," and started working up the courage to take your hand.

It was a long drive – the songs kept coming.

I thought it through, reached out and pulled your hand into my lap. I held it there for miles. The rush of the car was exhilarating. I began to take the corners with some speed, just because the car could.

I must have been occupied thinking about the fawn, or more likely about the dead body of the doe. Whatever I was thinking about, I was thinking hard because I didn't notice Grandfather at all. I was near the shed when he grabbed my wrist. He squeezed it very hard and pulled my arm up so that I had to stand on my toes. Then he didn't say anything. He just looked at me with a smirk, an ugly smirk.

Why didn't he say anything? Did he think I couldn't understand since I didn't talk? Strangely enough, I thought for a moment this was his idea of playing. So I started to smile. Instead of smiling back, he pulled up harder on my arm as if my smile meant he wasn't hurting me enough. Then in a slow quiet voice he said, "You had my gun down." He didn't say it with anger or to tell me I had done something wrong. No, it was more like, "You had my gun down. Now, what shall I do to you?"

What would you have expected me, or anyone for that matter, to do? To be obedient and take the pain? I couldn't, Philip. I could see no reason to accept what he was doing to me. If he had tried to explain why what I had done was wrong, then maybe I wouldn't have resented him so much, but he didn't say anything, Philip. He had no intention of reasoning with me. What else could I have done besides struggle to get away. That's what I did and even that didn't make him more serious. I'm afraid I hit him, Philip – not very hard. It was a tap really. I just brought my free hand up and struck his cheek. It shocked him. I'm sure of that. He tried to laugh it off as if it was all part of my ridiculous behaviour. I could see it upset him though. He wasn't expecting it.

I thought he would grab me again, so I waited there. When he didn't, I began backing away as if at any moment he might reach out for me. All that happened was I tripped over my own feet. Grandfather got a good laugh – it seems that's all he was looking for. He continued chuckling away and I could hear, "Stupid little kid. Stupid little kid," coming through his laugh.

The air was cooler when we emerged from the car at Niagara-on-the-Lake. Sally wanted to head for the first bar – you suggested a night stroll. When we passed our hotel, Ann said: "Jenny, you must be freezing. Come up and get a jacket." I insisted I was okay. Ann went up dragging Sally with her.

I was lost in a window display of porcelain dolls and Victorian dresses when you came up behind me. You put your lips close to my ear, "Ann and I have never slept together." I gave you a puzzled look. "We've just kissed, that's all." Your hand felt huge on the back of my neck. "What about Sally?" my voice quivered. I didn't mean it to, but it sounded like I was jealous. "Sally? Never." I smiled a smile of knowing. You saw a smile of acquiescence.

No sooner had you excused yourself to go to the men's room than Ann and Sally reappeared. "Has Philip gone up?" Ann drew on a practised look of disappointment. "I guess I brought your jacket down for nothing." Ann threw up her arms, "I think I'm going to go in myself."

Sally said she was going to the bar since you were paying. I took my jacket and said I'd walk a bit.

"Don't be out late," Ann said.

I'm surprised you didn't cross paths with her on your way out.

Sex was your moment. I'd never seen you so puffed up. My, the way you strutted around the room afterward. Then you came back for the long ride. There was a muffled rap on the door. It came again – you swelled.

The third time, I had to feed your penis into me.

You don't want to hear this, do you, Philip? Perhaps you don't even want to hear about the fawn. In all sincerity, I find it impossible to believe that anyone who is a half interested observer of the world would not want to hear what I have to say. But I'm keeping you from the story, am I not, Philip?

For a few days, I had brought the fawn milk to drink. I had spent an entire night fretting over how I was going to get the milk out of the house. In the morning I simply walked out the door with my glass and no one said anything. It drank the milk at first and I figured everything would be alright then. It would drink till it regained its strength and then it would go. On the third day when I entered the clearing, the milk was sour and the fawn was trembling and weak again. It couldn't even help itself, after all I had done for it and the risk I had taken stealing the milk. I was enraged. I walked right up and kicked it as hard as I could. It coward and trembled. When I moved, it shuddered.

I would be blamed. For sure the creature who lived in the clearing would think it was my fault. If it weren't for my coming and breaking in, none of this would have happened. I had to do something. I had to do something, Philip.

Quickly and in silence, I was gone. As soon as I was over the bank, I ran. My feet slapped through the stream dodging the stones. To think of it now makes me wonder how I didn't hurt myself. There were so many big and sharp stones. It didn't matter to me then, I was so furious. What I was doing I really hadn't considered. I was just doing it. That seems strange, doesn't it? After all, this wasn't some instant reaction, I had to run all the way back to the shed.

Instead of following the path and going through the back yard, I hopped a fence not far from the stream. This bit of property wasn't Grandfather's, but it had some trees and would help me sneak up on the shed. When I got there, I put my ear to the wall to make sure Grandfather was not inside. I would have to get in the door which was in plain view of the cottage. The thought of that made me scared and I was already scared enough. If they were in the kitchen, they might see me and Grandmother was probably already in there making lunch. I couldn't wait. So I ran to the door of the shed, turned the wooden latch, then opened and quickly pulled the door shut behind me. Needlessly, I held it tight shut and waited to be yelled at from across the back yard. I was almost positive that was it, that it was all over.

When I turned around and looked up the sight of the rifle hit me very hard. This was when I had the first doubts about what I was doing. I stood still, dead still. But no, as fearful as it may have been, I felt I had to do it. At that moment, I think I understood whether I did it or not, either way the result would be bad.

I couldn't stay still any longer. I got up onto the workbench knee first and grasped onto the rafters with one hand to lean out for the gun. It was such an awkward position to be in. I thought I would drop it. When I was standing on the floor holding the gun in my hands, I didn't even want to look at it. I just had to go and go quickly. From the drawer of the workbench, I took two bullets.

Leaving was obviously far more dangerous than getting into the shed, but I don't remember that part at all now, Philip. Once I had the gun all I felt was the pressure of getting back to the clearing.

I do remember the weight of the gun as I tried to run through the stream. I found it so heavy and it made me go slowly. My nervousness alone was making me breathless, but I struggled on. Passing by the falls, I felt so ashamed. I did not want to be noticed. I wanted to pretend the fawn wasn't there. In a moment, I would fix things up. If the falls would only be slow to look, it would be as if nothing had happened.

It was always hard to get up the bank – the gun made it no easier. In the forest, I was almost silent as I moved in straight toward the clearing. I saw the fawn from a good distance. It had no idea I was watching. Its tranquillity struck me. I thought it was a stupid senseless tranquillity. It must have known. Did it have no respect?

It didn't bother me to raise the rifle – I only pointed it vaguely in the fawn's direction.

Afterward, I marched straight back to the cottage and sat at the table and waited for lunch. Grandmother could see I looked determined and she knew something was up. After grace, I stuck my hand straight out and poked my finger into the sliced meat and I said, "Is that ham?"

All those years I confided in you, Philip. How many times had we been over it, all the possibilities. I said, "Maybe my mother was a drug addict." You said, "Maybe she was fighting an addiction." I said, "Maybe she had her own psychological problems." You said, "Yes, yes, Jenny, maybe she was struggling to find her own sense of equilibrium." I said, "How could she have left me?" and you said, "I don't know."

All along, you knew, you knew. My mother had been your patient before I was. Her leaving me was not the metaphysical conundrum, I wanted it to be. She abandoned me and you counselled her on how to feel okay about it.

I have a brother and a sister. Strange, I don't remember them.

It was even you, Philip, who played the decisive hand in the Betty affair – you signed the report recommending I be taken away from my grandparents.

Do you think I was capable of killing the fawn, Philip? It would have been the compassionate thing to do. It was so pathetic at the end. No, I didn't shoot it, though it was me who killed its mother.

Imagine the irony of it, Philip. You here in the Clarke, after all the years we spent in this building at our little weekly sessions. Now you're lying down, and I'm in the chair. The atmosphere is different. These hospital rooms are so sterile compared to your psychic boudoir of a consulting room downstairs with all its deep ochres and blood reds.

You know, it worked just like you explained it in your talk – one clean bullet shot through the left frontal lobe. You are part of a study now. Something about amino acid levels and frontal lobe injuries. That would make a good epitaph, don't you think? "Here lies a frontal lobe trauma subject with amino acid anomalies." Not that you're going to die soon. They say you might very well live for another ten years or fifteen even and that you can probably understand everything I say. Oh, I do hope so, Philip.

The police are calling it a botched suicide. In a real sense, it was. You were playing it, you were going to push it until it couldn't be pushed any further. The newspaper quoted a cop saying: "He was a doctor who studied the brain. I'd have thought he'd have known what he was doing. Maybe his hand slipped."

Around here, they can't help speculating you did it on purpose. In the hallways, they're recasting your life's work as one perverse odyssey to stamp out your own speech.

"Fiona, you shouldn't be out on the landing in your slip."

"Oh, Mummy." Fiona came back into the dressing room, her arms across her chest; she wanted to see who was at the door. She muttered under her breath, but smiled when Joseph, the old intelly, shook his head at her.

"I don't see why you can't wear the same dress all day," her mother said with a sigh of resignation.

"But, Mummy, Uncle Tice is coming and we're going to have dancing."

"We'll have to see what your Cousin Sally has to say about that."

"Uncle Tice will take care of Sally."

Mrs. McCauley cocked an eye at Fiona. She didn't like her daughter to speak that way in front of Joseph.

Mrs. McCauley went back to the wardrobe. "Try this on." She held out a dark dress with plenty of lace.

Fiona glared and fitted the dress over her head. "Oh, it's too frilly." She patted down the folds. "Besides, you know I wore this the last time Uncle Tice was here. I'm nineteen now, Mummy."

Fiona stepped aside and fingered the satin evening gown she had left there on the mannequin. "I could wear this green one."

"It's blue and blue doesn't become you."

"No, it isn't. It's green," Fiona retorted. "Joseph, what colour is this?"

"Mediterranean green, I would say, Miss Fiona."

Fiona looked at her mother as if to say, "You see."

Mrs. McCauley adjusted and pinched the dress to fit it to the mannequin. "It will take a lot of altering. I'm afraid Joseph just doesn't have the time."

"Please, Mummy."

"Joseph should be running the factory today. It's all he can do preparing for all this company."

"There's a line of jeans ending this morning. So I could fit it in. I'll do it on my hour, Ma'am," Joseph offered, keen as ususal to please Fiona.

"Oh, would you, Joseph?" Fiona waited on her mother's answer.

"All right, all right."

Fiona jumped at Joseph. She kissed his white beard and whispered: "Now you can send the information to Uncle Tice from the factory."

Joseph's face suddenly went white. He calmly answered: "Yes, Fiona."

"What are you on about now?" Mrs. McCauley asked.

"The dress, Mummy, it will be glorious."

"Not a word about this to anyone." Isadora McCauley sensed they were not listening to her and so she tried to sound stern. "You know what people are always saying about making intellies work on their hour." Fiona had already pulled a terminal from its hiding place in the wall and handed Joseph a wand to take her measurements. As Mrs. McCauley left the room, she turned a suspicious eye on the dress: it would be the first time her daughter would show her shoulders in public and that bothered her far more than what anyone might say about an intelly being overworked.

"Hello, Cousin Eliza." Fiona strolled across the living room. "A kiss, Eliza." She held her cheek next to her cousin's.

Eliza, being single, always arrived early and she was happy to let everyone know she had had to entertain herself.

"I'm sorry we weren't here to greet you," Mrs. McCauley said flatly, following Fiona in, "with so many people coming we have a lot of preparations."

"Yes, especially for Uncle Tice. What time do you expect him down from Toronto?"

"You know your Uncle Tice." Mrs. McCauley left it at that.

"I couldn't help noticing, Isadora," Eliza said with an affectation that put Mrs. McCauley on her guard, "that the furniture had been pushed back."

"Yes," Mrs. McCauley explained, "Henry had Joseph make a little space in case any of the guests wanted to dance."

"Oh, indeed," Eliza had nothing better to say – Mrs. McCauley had stolen her thunder by raising the issue of dancing so bluntly.

"Doesn't it make for a lovely large space," Fiona said in a detached tone.

Eliza ignored her cousin and addressed her aunt: "I hate to alarm you, Isadora," she said in anything but a consoling voice, "your floor is slanted. I swear it must be an inch lower there by the inner wall."

"Three quarters," Mrs. McCauley retorted. "Unfortunately, we didn't notice it until after the other renovations had been done. Joseph is going to fix it, but it will have to wait until his apprentice at the factory becomes more independent."

"Yes, these big old houses got terribly run down while they were neglected for so long," Eliza went on. "But I see you've restored the veranda wonderfully."

"Yes, hasn't Joseph designed it well?"

"Tell me, Isadora, is it true that intellies used to live here?"

"There are rumours."

"The people in Glencoe say they remember hundreds of them living right here in this house. They were just squatting, of course. They used it as some sort of conference centre."

"Where can Henry be?" Mrs. McCauley said with perturbation.

"He was here to let me in," Eliza offered.

"Fiona, go find your father." Mrs. McCauley added to Eliza: "Would you care to help me get some drinks?"

"Where is Joseph?" Eliza asked not too innocently.

"He's on his hour. He offered to take it early, so I gave him two."

In the front hall, Fiona heard Lester's car arrive. She pushed back the curtain – she was fascinated. Her father was on his way out to greet them. Sally got out and tidied herself, while Lester told the intelly driver when to return for them. Nobody but Lester in these parts had a car. He had gone to some trouble to get it and even more for permission to use it on the roads. Finally, he got a medical certificate to say Sally couldn't fly. People said he bought it from a doctor who'd been known to trade on the intelly black market. Lester and her father were shaking hands now. They stepped back to admire the car then Lester opened the hood and they both hung over the engine a while.

Lester loved to ride the country roads. For years he had gone out on the farm transports with the intellies. Now that he had inherited much of the farmland in the area, he felt even more of a need to get out and trace the property. This was good farmland. It was shameful to see so many rundown homes and the potholed roads. His grandfather had said that in his day the whole area had been prosperous on tobacco money. Mile after mile of tree-lined flat land with big homes and rows of kilns in the yards. Lester had hope for the area now that it was becoming popular again with people moving out from the city. He could see a day when the intellies were contained, the homes restored and boating returned to the Thames.

Leaving the men outside, Sally came into the living room and looked around, just as Eliza had done. Mrs. McCauley and Eliza arrived with a tray of drinks.

Sally took one politely, "Lemonade, Aunt Isadora?"

"Why yes, of course, Sally."

"Are you too serving the drinks, Eliza?" Sally asked her sister.

Mr. McCauley cut in, "I just spoke to Joseph. He's on his way to the factory."

"To the factory," Eliza said as if this couldn't be possible, "On his hour?"

"Yes," Mr. McCauley answered good humouredly, "he's doing a little something for Fiona on his own time. He's so sweet on her."

Mrs. McCauley made a mental note to have a word with her husband.

"You really ought to have more intellies, Isadora," Sally said.

"Joseph takes care of all our needs."

"How can he," Sally commented patronizingly, "with this big house?"

"I thought one was all that was allowed?"

"Yes, that's fine if you live in a little condo, like you did in the city. But out here? Joseph is away all day at the factory and you could use two intellies just to run this house, let alone do all the renovations and up-keep on the grounds."

Sally somehow had to justify their three intellies since their house wasn't half the size of the McCauley's. She had got her first extra by saying she needed one for housework and Lester had got one for his car; of course, the chauffeur did other things when he wasn't driving.

Eliza nudged Isadora – a smile escaping from her lips, "Lester is applying to breed intellies."

Sally looked at her sister as though she were chastising a child for letting out secrets.

Left on her own, Sally turned her head in a dramatic sweeping gaze of the cleared floor space. She, like Eliza, may have wanted to ask why the space had been created, but Fiona came in: "I wonder when Uncle Tice will arrive?"

"Fiona, darling," Sally went to her and pulled the girl's head forward to kiss her on the brow. "Delighted to see you, dear."

"Fiona," Lester had arrived; his voice boomed. He was considered a man of some importance in the area. "It's always a pleasure to see such a sweet young face," he added, half speaking to Mr. McCauley.

Fiona curtsied.

"Lester, you and that car of yours," Mr. McCauley slapped Lester on the back. "I was at the factory the other day going over the records." Mrs. McCauley cleared her throat. Mr. McCauley went on: "I noticed a lot of delays in the deliveries. 'Joseph,' I said, 'what is the meaning of this?' and Joseph says, 'That's Lester, Sir. Every time he goes out in his limousine all the traffic around here has to stop.'"

"Those intellies, they'll use any excuse," Lester said. Mr. McCauley laughed and Lester returned a chuckle of avoidance. It was difficult to tell if he did it to disguise the boost to his ego or to cover his embarrassment.

"Is that a limousine we've got?" Sally asked quizzically, "I thought it was a Ford."

Mrs. McCauley brought drinks to the men and drew her husband aside. "One of these days Lester is going to ask to see your records and then you'll be stuck."

Sally and Lester seated themselves. It was obvious they found the arrangement of the furniture peculiar. For the moment they said nothing. It was clear they felt discomforted at the prospect of speaking to their hosts across the room.

To forestall more uncomfortable questions about dancing, Mrs. McCauley took her husband by the hand and went to sit beside Sally.

"You've done a wonderful job on the house," Lester complimented, running his eyes across the ceiling.

"Why, thank you," Mr. McCauley said as though it were unexpected.

"How long has it been now that you've been here?" Lester asked.

"One year," Mr. McCauley said plainly.

"Yes," Sally cut in, "it was about this time last year when Uncle Tice was down that we came to see it." She said this as though she had to search her memory to recall the event.

"You've done very well," Lester said nodding his head approvingly – he was leading up to something more important. "What we need is for more good conservative people like you to move into the area."

"Lester," Mrs. McCauley said in a reprimanding, but good-hearted tone, "we moved here because we like it the way it is."

"Yes, keeping it like it is. How often I've said just that to Sally." His wife complied. "I believe that with a few more people we could control the bad intelly elements which are ruining this area."

"How's that?" Mrs. McCauley asked.

"Well, there is a law which allows people to form a local government."

"I thought it was a municipal government?" Sally cut in again. "Isn't that what you had the intellies look up?"

"Yes, very true, very true, Sally," Lester acknowledged, "a municipal government of Thamesville. With a government we could protect the conservative way of life here."

"We didn't leave the city because we are conservatives," Mrs. McCauley said defensively. "We just didn't like the city anymore."

"Oh, I know," Lester was emphatic. "So many good people are turning their backs on what the liberals have done to the city."

"It sounds like you want to bring the city out here, Lester, and we don't like the city."

Lester spoke at length about how he would clean up Thamesville and the surrounding area. "It's not right, Lester said as though espousing the authority of a natural law, "that people should have intellies as neighbours."

"Like most of the people in Glencoe," Eliza said, "some of the intellies are better off than they are."

Mrs. McCauley took offense: "I suppose, Lester, you would include Joseph's apprentice in this clean-up."

"Isadora," Sally laid a hand on her aunt's arm, "when Joseph dies the apprentice will live here in Joseph's room, won't he? So there is no problem. Is there? You should have him here now anyway. You need more than one intelly."

"Your apprentice is really no problem," Lester tried to sound reassuring, "it's the free intellies who should be watched. In my opinion there shouldn't be any intellies living on their own, they should all be working. You never know what they're up to with all their free time. We all know what too much free time has led to in the past."

"There aren't any free intellies in the city," Fiona said forcefully from across the room as though she were trying to make Lester understand.

"Now, Fiona," Lester said, "that's not quite true and with the spread of liberalism there'll be more of it."

"It is true that many do live on their own in the city," Mr. McCauley broke in with the voice of reason, "but there aren't any free intellies, they all work for someone."

Everyone nodded, as though happy the disagreement had been resolved.

"Yes, Fiona," Lester said, "you are quite right to correct me. And it could soon be the same way here."

"I've heard there are whole cities of free intellies out west," Eliza said with wonder, "and they're rich, richer than us even."

Everyone laughed and Fiona took the opportunity to nip out because she'd heard Joseph come in through the back door.

Lester went on describing how certain intellies were living on prime land in the heart of Thamesville and acting as though they owned it. In the kitchen, Fiona was raising a commotion, which Lester insisted on speaking up against. He then got onto how this new municipal government would regulate deeds of ownership for every property within the boundaries of Thamesville.

The noise finally ended with Fiona running up the back stairway. Then Joseph appeared.

"Where was I?" Lester said.

"Joseph, could you get me another lemonade?" Sally held up her glass.

Joseph took Sally's glass and nodded. He then stepped into the kitchen and a moment later a self-propelled trolley with an urn came out and poured and presented Sally a glass.

"Life would be so much simpler when Joseph isn't around, if that machine and I could get along." Mrs. McCauley raised her chin at the trolley.

"It's very simple to use, Ma'am," Joseph said, "I could show you how."

"Yes, Joseph, I know you've offered a thousand times, but these things and I just don't get along."

"You see, now, Isadora," Sally reprimanded, "if you had that apprentice here, you wouldn't be stuck serving drinks yourself."

"Oh, no, he has to stay at the factory. He's there more than Joseph even."

"The 'he' is a she, Ma'am," Joseph corrected.

Lester looked up, taken aback by Joseph speaking. He turned to Mr. McCauley: "Henry, I hope you've had her fixed."

"Lester," there was anxiety in Mrs. McCauley's voice, "you know that's against the law."

"Yes, yes, I know, but all you need is a consent."

"If she doesn't ask, we won't ask her," Mrs. McCauley

spoke with a sharp edge to her voice. "Coercion is also against the law, you know." The conversation paused and only the nervous shifting of Eliza's feet attracted attention. Mrs. McCauley spoke again with a tone of reconciliation: "Lester, for a man who is so quick to impose the law, you sure can find ways to get around it."

Lester grinned like a fat cat and Mrs. McCauley smiled back.

"I'm surprised at you, Isadora," Sally spoke up, "not knowing this intelly was a girl. "Didn't you interview her?"

"No, should we? Joseph took care of it."

"You shouldn't leave such a thing to a intelly," Sally said, "they are so in with their own kind."

"This intelly could be living with you for the next sixty years," Eliza said in shock, "and you don't even know who she is."

"Now," Mr. McCauley said, hoping to sound a note of finality, "Joseph has been with my family for as long as I can remember. He cares for us better than we can ourselves."

"Yes, Joseph?" Mrs. McCauley reflected on how the old intelly always seemed to sense the appropriate moment to let some fact be known.

"Dale is arriving."

"Wonderful," Mrs. McCauley said rising from her seat. How did Joseph know about these things? He always spoke about "the monitors," but since it had become fashionable to disguise them, Mrs. McCauley could no longer discern when something was up. Even when she had seen them, she couldn't comprehend the gibberish they produced. Fiona though, bless her soul, could understand them.

"Where is Dale, Joseph?" Mrs. McCauley asked.

"He'll be coming by way of the front door, Ma'am."

"He wants to check out the veranda," Mr. McCauley laughed. "He doesn't trust Joseph."

Mrs. McCauley's eyes inflamed. She resented her husband's letting it out that Dale did this sort of thing.

After descending from putting on her dress, Fiona had waited in the front hall, preferring to listen in to the conversation in the living room and not be seen. When everyone came out to meet Dale, she was about to throw open the doors, but Sally shouted: "Oh, my," and ran her fingertips along Fiona's collar bone.

"Now, Fiona pay no attention to Sally," Lester said, "it's a beautiful dress for a beautiful young lady."

Finally, Fiona flung open the front doors and the assembled party found themselves face to face with Dale out on the lawn looking up critically toward the house. Fiona skipped across the wooden veranda and down the steps ahead of them.

"Fiona," Dale kissed his sister.

Fiona held her brother by the shoulders and spoke into his ear: "I sent the information."

"What information?" Dale would have interrogated her further but Mr. McCauley started the group laughing as he was so proud of himself for having predicted what Dale was up to.

After everyone had come down to greet him, Dale returned to his examination of the veranda. He threw a few guarded questions at Joseph about the specifications. Joseph shrugged like he didn't know the answers. All the other renovations had been passed by Dale for approval and he was maddened that the same hadn't been done for the veranda. He wouldn't have been nearly as perturbed if it didn't look so grand.

Mrs. McCauley took her favourite by the arm and demanded Joseph get him something to drink.

"Rye, Joseph," Dale said warmly, showing that he was past being vexed.

"Really, Dale, you drink that stuff?" Sally said. Her shock was so affected it made everyone laugh.

"Now, it may be an intoxicant, Sally, but at least it's a good local drink," Lester's humour sounded sincere.

Everyone followed Dale and his mother as they strolled arm in arm into the living room.

"No, here, Dale," Mrs. McCauley said pointing out an armchair. She took the rye from Joseph and handed it to her son.

"Dale, did you see Thamesville as you flew over?" Sally asked.

"Yes, good old Thamesville," Dale said.

"Myself and a group of concerned citizens," Lester spoke with some gravity, "are seriously considering forming a local government here."

"Is that so?" Dale erased his smile.

"It's really only the abuses of the intellies that are making this necessary," Lester said.

"Oh," Dale looked surprised, "what sort of abuses?"

Sally explained: "You know, squatting and the regular sort of thing – tobacco." Before *the big freeze* people in the area had grown a drug called tobacco. The intellies had revived the practice, hiding the plants in amongst the crops and selling it for exorbitant prices on the black market. The intellies were having some success in corrupting youths with it. It was said that nicotine, a substance in the tobacco, made children think too much and use their imaginations.

"Have you reported this to the police?"

"Yes, we've tried that route," Lester said, "but I'm afraid the infection of liberalism has spread there too."

Dale nodded. To fill the pause Sally said: "You know, the police and the intellies have their little arrangements, black market, that sort of thing."

"Lester, I'm glad you're doing something about it," Dale tried to humour him. "When is Uncle Tice arriving?"

The last time Uncle Tice was down he and Lester had clashed over Tice's liberal views on intellies; it was all polite of course. Mrs. McCauley had been glad to hear Sally say they would come this time knowing Tice would be there. Then again, Tice was such an important man in the Corporation, Lester could hardly afford not to show up.

The last occasion was when the McCauleys had invited everyone to see the house and its magnificent property. The central structure was built just after the war with the Americans and it had had some additions during the period of the underground railroad, in which, it is said, the house played a significant role. After that, its history was a little clouded: for the past generation perhaps, it had been squatted in by intellies. And there it sat, a little north of Thamesville, waiting to be restored.

Joseph had erected a tent out on the lawn as the interior really wasn't liveable. Tice was going on about making life better for the intellies, more housing, some health care. No one there had ever heard anyone talk like that before. They knew it was only his position that protected him. Lester was not one to let such things pass and he went at Tice head on:

"Are there not people in the Corporation like yourself, Tice, who are really like the intellies, people who have and cultivate the knowledge of technology?"

Tice did not avoid the question: "It is necessary that some people have to continue their learning in order to know what it is that the intellies are doing and to instruct them properly. As you know, not being practically minded, they would be off on tangents and not serving the utility of the people. The role of the corporate citizen is not unlike that of the doctors, lawyers or engineers; like Dale, some people take it on as their duty to continue learning, not because they like knowledge but because we would be at the mercy of the intellies if someone didn't."

"With the professions that's different," Lester was prepared. "They are learning scientifically to acquire specific and limited knowledge; they are not just learning. Tice, as you admit, with people in the administration doing learning like the intellies, don't you think that breeds a level of tolerance – letting this and that abuse go because you want to portray a stance of understanding? Isn't that what's leading to an environment of revolt and even revolution?"

"You're right, Lester. There have been problems in the past with little groups of intellies getting out of hand, sabotaging facilities and creating viruses, and, of course, there was *the big freeze* when all the computers were connected, but without administrators in the Corporation who understand what the intellies are doing, we would be at even greater risk. But intellies getting out of hand and taking liberties is not the problem – revolt among the intellies is misunderstood. They are happy to serve. It is actually their living conditions and the denial of basic rights and abuse that is the cause of revolt and treachery on their part."

Lester looked down at the grass: "I've heard talk from very good sources that there is a movement afoot to foment a full scale revolution by the intellies with the help of people in the Corporation."

Tice laughed and everyone joined in. "Well, if there was, I would know about it. It's okay, Lester," Tice sounded casually patronizing, "you can sleep at night. There is no such movement."

Mrs. McCauley, afraid that the conversation was going down the same old road again, told herself that she should start talking about flowers and gardening, but she just couldn't help herself: "Seriously, Lester, you can't tell the wind to stop blowing – intellies have been squatting in Thamesville for as long as I can remember."

"That's true," Lester admitted, "but whenever someone needed the space, you didn't have to say a word and they were gone. Now, they think they have a right to property and there are people living in worse accommodations than some intellies. With a strong conservative government here, we could put a stop to this."

"Lester," Dale said point-blankly, "I'm no liberal, but you have to admit that liberalism does have its merits."

Lester pondered, forcing Dale to wait on an answer: "Perhaps that depends on your point of view."

"How can anyone deny all the innovations the intellies have brought about. If we hadn't given them their hour, society would be twenty years behind. When people were running the computers, how far did we get? I know that many of the intellies started out as hackers sabotaging systems, but that's the past. Let's look ahead. In my field, engineering, the private research of intellies has made all the difference. You know, Lester, by law, they're not required to share any of their findings with us."

"As you say, I'm sure these innovations are a great boost to your field, but the intellies have made us think too much about technical things. It may be very convenient to pop up and down from London on your private craft, but flying, you know, is unnatural. The intellies have made us stress advancement over human values. Many of these innovations really came about because the intellies didn't want to do the work and so they invented something to do it for them. Consequently, we have free intellies. Many of whom are living in poverty. Perhaps we should set aside some of their innovations and allow them all to be employed."

"As I said, Lester, I'm no liberal, but I know a good thing when I see it. If we've been so stodgy as to let a few conveniences corrupt our values, then it's our own fault. Many intellies work very hard. If some of them are getting ahead because of it, I don't think we should hold it against them."

"Oh, absolutely," Lester said.

"Absolutely," Sally echoed.

"That's just my point, Dale. There's no doubt about it," Lester went on. "Many intellies do deserve better, but we can't allow a situation to arise where people are put out for the sake of intellies. As you know, it is not always those intellies who deserve more, who have more."

Mr. McCauley stepped into the room and announced: "Bertrand and his wife are on their way over."

"Oh, good," Mrs. McCauley got up, "why don't we go out to the veranda." She turned to Lester and Sally. "You know our neighbour, Bertrand and his wife, don't you?"

"Yes, I believe we met once," Lester said.

On the veranda, Mrs. McCauley hurriedly introduced Bertrand to the rest of her company and chastised Joseph because the drinks weren't being served properly.

Dale took Fiona by the hand and said he needed to have another look at the veranda. Out on the lawn looking up and pointing toward the house he asked: "What information did you send, Fiona?"

"The information we collected on Lester for Uncle Tice," Fiona said, as though it were obvious.

"The entire file?" Dale swallowed. "How did you send it?"

"I had Joseph send it from the factory."

"He did that?"

"Don't worry, it would have gone out among the factory invoices. There's no monitoring."

Dale climbed the steps back up onto the veranda, trying not to show his distress.

Mr. McCauley was attempting to bring his neighbour into the conversation: "We've just been talking about living conditions in Thamesville."

"Terrible, terrible," Bertrand muttered.

Lester perked up. "What do you think can be done about it?"

"Well, I suppose better housing for the intellies."

There was a pause in the conversation.

"Lester," Dale spoke up, "has been telling us that some people in Thamesville are worse off than certain intellies."

"Unfortunately, the only solution to that is to raise the intelly tax," Bertrand said and quickly lifted his glass.

"That would work, Bertrand, but . . ."

"I've said it before," Mrs. McCauley sounded aggravated, "I don't think that those of us who employ intellies profitably should have to pay for those who don't."

"Don't you think, Bertrand," Lester said, "a more practical solution would be for the intellies who are squatting on good property to give it up?"

"Yes," Bertrand stared into his glass, "very practical."

"Then there would be more room for conservatives," Eliza said with excitement.

Fiona looked about for Joseph. There was nothing here

for her to drink. Her father and brother could drink alcohol in full sight of everyone, but her mother would not allow her the prerogative. So, whenever anyone was around, she would send Joseph to fetch her a drink with a little colour. She found Joseph, but he was getting some instructions from her mother. Fiona waited, then seeing the old intelly leave, she called: "Joseph," and extended her glass. She was too late.

Sally sidled up to her and said: "Why don't you ask Bertrand's wife to get you a drink?"

Fiona pursed her lips. She wanted to walk away, but Sally was standing so close to her it would have been like breaking an intimacy. Fiona could feel Sally's breath on her neck and shoulders – she wanted to cover herself up.

"I wish I was your age," Sally said with envy. "Then again, you'll probably be as old as me before you're married."

"Sally, really."

"Oh, you think you stand a chance against all those *free* intelly girls."

"Sally, where do you dredge up such ugly gossip?"

"Ugly gossip? Do you think Dale and Tice are living like bachelors up in the city? They probably tell their intelly girls, 'After the revolution, I'll marry you.'"

Fiona left Sally there laughing to herself.

"I've only been in this part of the country to visit my folks, Lester," Dale was saying. "I don't know the town as well as you do, but if conditions for the intellies are as you say they are, it's a wonder more of them don't move into the area."

"I'm afraid they will."

Dale ignored the comment for the moment. "Things aren't like this everywhere, you know. In fact, Thamesville must be an exception. I had a contract in a town near Windsor where the living conditions for the intellies are abominable. Most of them actually live on the street. It makes the town so unsightly. You'd think the people would provide some housing or give the intellies a quarter where they could build for themselves."

From the lawn, Joseph signalled to Mr. McCauley that Tice was approaching. There was a cheerful reaction when it was suggested everyone move around the house to welcome Tice.

The party strolled across the side lawn to where the landing pad was concealed. A warm sou'wester was passing and, for the time being, everyone forgot their arguments. Fiona straggled along at the rear. She wondered what Tice would say to her. She wished Lester and Sally hadn't come, then everyone wouldn't have to spend the day meddling in someone else's politics, and she would get much more attention from Uncle Tice. Anyway, her Papa had promised there would be dancing – Sally, or no Sally.

The company was making its way between the gigantic Mesopotamian spruces. The poor trees now had to compete for grandeur with the house, but when Fiona had first seen the place, these straight and massive things were the only sign of a former opulence. Papa maintained that Mother had chosen the house just for these trees. Sally, Eliza and Lydia, Bertrand's wife, were holding up their dresses in the long grass as they passed around the low boughs. Sally was such a snob; it surprised Fiona to see her talking to Lydia in an animated manner. Mother said that Lydia had arrived at a function once wearing her jeans. She was newly emancipated then and wasn't worried about losing her status.

Lester had drifted over to talk with the women. He had

a little repartee going with Lydia. Fiona didn't want to hear it and so she had stayed back near the spruces. There was always a breeze cutting through here – a gentle whistle – it seemed to drive her back into childhood. The men were standing cross-armed. Joseph had signalled that Tice was late, then he shrugged from time to time to suggest that he didn't know what was up when Dale or Mr. McCauley raised a chin at him.

Finally, Mr. McCauley told Joseph to find out what was happening. Everyone watched as the old intelly keyed in a message on the panel at the landing station. Fiona wondered if it was really taking that long – Joseph was getting slow in his reactions. He seemed quick enough, though, when he grabbed a headset and began talking with someone. "Are you sure?" they all heard him yell into the headset.

To everyone's surprise, Dale ran up and lifted the headset right off of Joseph. He listened in, pressing his finger tips against the earpiece because of the wind, but he didn't say a word. Then he ripped the headset off letting it fall to the ground and ran up to the house.

Joseph came up to Mr. McCauley, stepping cautiously in the long grass, and looking older than ever: "It's Tice, Sir, he has been arrested."

LEAH AND RACHEL

The delights of the Tuscan town are many and Nick was determined to find them all. He wasn't sure about the church of Valdottavo, but better an affront to his senses, he thought, than a pleasure lost. The church on the cliff with all its white Carrara marble seemed alluring and at the same time repulsive for reasons he could not quite put his finger on. Maybe he would summon up the strength to make the trek up there, but then again, maybe not. Perhaps he should find Perchin, get his business over with and get out.

He looked from the church to the main street and spat on the ground. Another smoke and a coffee in front of the tavern would do he thought. Then he heard the organ – only a few base notes carried in the humid morning air; it was Sunday. In his indecision he looked down. The earth had absorbed his spit: his mother said that meant a place would accept you; and so with a little smile he slipped his cigarettes back into the pocket of his jacket and began the climb up to the church.

As he reached the top, Nick had to tell himself to breathe deeply. It was not that he was in such bad shape for a young man; he knew his breathlessness had been brought on by the thought of meeting Perchin. He leaned back against the balustrade and took a few moments to calm his heart, looking up as he did at the church in all its white shimmering and hard marble splendour. He could see what had brought on his consternation over the architectural integrity of the building: the fine baroque porch and side aisle, in all their precise angularity, had been hooked onto a lofty gothic nave like some whitewashed cubist rectangle painted over a masterwork.

Mass was on inside and it seemed dark until his eyes adjusted. It surprised him that this arrival caused no stir amongst the local churchgoers. Ten kilometres from Lucca and populated with *maisons secondaires,* perhaps Valdottavo was used to visitors. There was a hubbub in the congregation that made Nick feel welcome and at the same time made him wonder how the old priest could tolerate it. Such activity, the women coming and going from the candles and the statue of St Anthony, was not something one would expect to find in Toronto anymore. Taking in all these distractions, Nick hardly noticed the baldheaded man gesticulating to him. As Nick approached, the man slid his children down the pew like shuffle board weights and Nick smiled and nodded as if he understood.

The priest droning on, the children, the noise, all provided a strangely comforting backdrop for Nick to settle in and watch the ritual. In the shadows, his eyes searched the sombre paintings of the side chapels. Like many of these big village churches half the pews had been removed. Those that were left were full and so this tight congregation sat in an immense sense of space and height with the sun filtering in on them from the upper windows. It was a setting conducive to contemplation and Nick let his mind wander from old woman to young man to single mother wondering why it was that even in this village people worshipped separately from their families. Near the front of the church he spotted the exception. A father and daughter sat in the second row with the mother and elder daughter standing stiffly and precisely behind them. The tall and still blond curly haired man would periodically twist to see if the mother and daughter had strayed out of alignment. He was gaunt, wiry and stoney blue-eyed – it had to be Perchin: how many German families could there be in this town.

The wife was tall and fair too and in her demeanor at least seemed a natural companion to the older daughter beside her. But the daughters were dark haired and on the shorter side. Of the daughter in front all Nick could catch was the shoulders and head, a beautiful oval head; it looked most familiar. Nick took off his jacket and slid down closer to the children to see if he could get a better view of her, folding his jacket as he did and laying it on the pew beside him. They talked amongst themselves; the man, whom Nick took for Perchin, leaning his pasty and pock-marked face down to the daughter and she, in a black suit, holding her poise and speaking straight ahead as though to God. Nick waited, anticipating that at some point she would fully expose her profile. Next to her father, the skin of her cheek appeared to reflect an olive tone.

The sound of buttons skidding across the pew caught Nick's attention: one of the *bambini* had sent his jacket flying. He looked up to the front quickly enough to see Perchin's daughter turn. It was her, the girl, with the emerald nose stud he'd seen the day before at the Pensione Cancello where he was staying.

He'd come down for a beer to quench his thirst from the trip. She was at the bar with three boys; all of them pushing twenty, all dressed the same in jeans and tops that left their shoulders bare. Like Nick, they waited for beer; there was a lot of noise from a party in the next room. The boys began calling out, *"Birra, birra."* Nick assumed they were regulars and this was all in jest and so Nick too called out, "*Birra*," trying to mimic their Italian. They laughed and raised their empty glasses, "*Cin cin*."

"*Cin cin*," Nick saluted them back.

"*Americano?*" a blond boy with a magnificent grin called out to Nick.

"No, no, Dino," the girl spoke in the sweetest voice, "he is not American."

Nick admired her English.

Just then a door flew opened next to him revealing the festive dinner table. The hotel owner was struggling to come through with a beer cask which Nick helped him roll behind the bar, the two of them bumping shoulder-to-shoulder as they went. Nick won a big pat on the back and cheers from the boys and Perchin's daughter leaned over the bar to kiss him and the owner, old man Cancello.

Nick was still searching for her face through the rows of parishioners in the church when he noticed the elder sister staring back at him. She was a little heavier, slightly shorter; she was off-putting. Yet Nick wasn't exactly sure what it was about her. He couldn't tell what she looked like under her box-like dark clothing. She seemed strangely neutral; maybe it was the Nana Mouskouri glasses.

To break off from her stare, Nick looked up. The central pillars of the church were not stone, nor faced in marble, they were brick. It seemed that not only did the building live in the Baroque and Gothic, but the vault of the transept was even earlier; it was Romanesque. It had neither the beautiful curves and points of the soaring nave, nor the order of the marble chapels; it was a little rustic and squat, but its rounded arches held him like the reflection of an orderly and intelligent mind set in something immoveable.

Before Nick realized what had happened the mass had ended. People were streaming out and turning their backs on the old priest even before he disappeared behind the sanctuary. Nick was craning his neck to see where Perchin's younger daughter had got to when he felt an annoying tug on his shirt sleeve. *"Turista? Turista?"*

"No, no," Nick smiled at the man who had invited him into the pew.

"Business?" The man asked in perfect, if studied, English. His children crowded round, all staring up at Nick for an answer.

"Yes," replied Nick, "business."

"What kind of business?"

Nick shrugged his shoulders. What did he say now? They were waiting for an answer. Even the little mischievous-faced four-year-old was holding out for an answer.

"Perchin," Nick said, not knowing what else to offer them.

"Aaah, Mister Perchin."

"Mister Perchin," an echo came from several rows away.

Nick thought he should extricate himself, *"Buon giorno,"* he said and forced his way into the aisle.

The priest dressed in a beat-up tiara hat had somehow slipped around to the main doors. He was creating a bottle neck, insisting on shaking the hand of every parishioner. Feeling claustrophobic, Nick pushed his way through with only a smile to the priest, but as he stepped out into the sunlight he was tripped up by a voice feigning familiarity.

"Nick, Nick." The voice came with the stress on the 'k'. Claus Perchin towered over him on the stairs and took Nick's hand in both of his.

"Your mother, Nick, how is she?" Perchin didn't wait on an answer, he turned to Nick's pew mate, "My cousin, my mother's cousin's son." The man had evidently wasted no time in making Nick's presence known.

"*Cugino*?" the man lowered his eyebrows, a friendly reprimand for Nick.

"When did you get in?" Perchin was sounding paternal.

The answer, "Just now," was on Nick's lips when he saw the black outline of Perchin's younger daughter come through the crowd; the emerald catching the sun. Instead, Nick found himself saying: "Yesterday. I got in yesterday afternoon."

Until that moment Nick had forgotten the words his mother had relayed about her cousin Katrina's family: "She has two granddaughters. She says she loves them both dearly, but says the elder one, Leah, "is an odious thing" and the younger one, Rachel, "is an angel, an angel without volition . . . isn't that a strange thing to say." His mother had gone on about the daughters, but Nick had been absorbed by her comments on Perchin's business acumen: "Katrina says the locals call him, 'the man who makes oil from olive pits.'"

"Good to see you, Rachel, is it?" Nick said.

"Good to see you, Nick, is it?" she said half mockingly, half in fun.

It was the same warm voice and delicate accent that had played in Nick's mind since he had met her at the bar. He returned a guarded smile, not so much to conceal anything from Perchin, as from the mother standing behind. This was the first real look Nick had had of the older woman's face and he was surprised at how sunken and gray her eyes were. All the time she stood there, she seemed on the verge of saying something.

"My wife, Veronica," Perchin said. Then he slipped down to the step Nick was on. "You must come and stay with us." Perchin pointed out a house down the valley and tried to trace the outline of a road curving up the hillside. Nick squinted, unable to bring the hill into focus, until he realized that the tiny flicker he saw moving across the hill was a car appearing and disappearing amongst the trees.

"Don't worry," Perchin said, "Leah will come to collect you," and he called for his elder daughter. Nick could see there was something about Leah's smirk that could make a grandmother suspicious, but he could not find anything positively odious. She came right up to him and kissed him graciously and, when she stepped back, left a pleasant scent. It was agreed she would call at the hotel in an hour to bring him to the house and they would dine together.

On his way down the steps Nick heard: "I told you he was here," but wasn't sure which of the women had said it. He was hoping for a wave or even the suggestion of a smile from Rachel, but she had gone. Perchin was the only one left and he was speaking, sternly it seemed, to the priest. Far from being taken aback by Perchin's words, the old priest nodded keenly in a half-mad grin.

After returning to his hotel room, Nick found himself by the bed holding up the lid of his suitcase; he went through it again. Everything was in there. But it seemed lighter than it should be, something was missing. He went to check the closet again. He checked his watch – forty-five minutes. He had to figure things out. Just his jacket in the closet. He thought of Rachel. She seemed happy to see him at the church. The day before she had stood by quietly, smiling and quiet, while those boys goofed around at the bar. After they had got their beer, they had all sat out on the terrace. Nick, to his side, pretended to mind his own business. Rachel was talking to her friends in Italian, and Nick could make out that they were teasing her. Then she had spoken up in English, clearly for Nick's benefit: "No, I never do want to be sarcastic. I want to look at life honestly, straight on."

Nick closed up the suitcase. He needed a drink, a drink and a smoke. He had to figure things out; he had to figure Perchin out. As he signed, he asked for a Suze; something bitter was the right antidote for the ache in his stomach. Glass in hand, he went out to the front of the hotel to wait, taking a seat in the shade.

Perchin would eat him alive; that was the truth. What had his mother been thinking of when she put him in touch with that man? Nick thought about his staff working away at the office in Toronto and felt vaguely responsible. He'd never really thought of himself as their guardian before, but now he feared the contract with Perchin would be their demise. The Suze, imbibed slowly, felt good going down. He thought about Rachel. If he was going to lose his company, he certainly was not going to leave without Rachel.

A big black Mercedes was coming down the deserted noon street toward the hotel. Nick stood to light another cigarette. After one long drag he flung it to the ground, finished the Suze, and put on his sunglasses. The car kind of rumbled and rolled toward him in its own good time; the dark outlines of Leah's glasses clearly visible through the windshield. As she turned the car around, Leah offered Nick a limp wave. He approached, wondering if her smirky smile ever left her lips; it wasn't a child's empty smirk, not one a rebuke could wipe away, it was a look of knowing. Nick bet she did know all about him and his little business and his contract problems and a whole lot more. He held his hand up to cover the view of her mouth and nose – even her eyes smirked.

When he got close to the car, Leah slid over into the passenger's seat, and Nick took the cue opening the driver's door. "What about my rental?" he asked.

"Cancello will watch it for you. Don't worry." Nick turned just in time to see the old man in the doorway giving Leah a perfunctory nod of agreement. Then she added: "I'll drop you back sometime to pick it up."

When Nick got in she leaned not too far his way and tapped her cheek for a kiss. "You'll have to pay attention, it's complicated getting out of the village," Nick wondered if she was patronizing him, but she went on, "if you ever get lost, line up the church bell tower with the one across the valley and you'll find the road. It's just outside the village."

"You sound Canadian," Nick said.

"Yes, I'm the only one the accent stuck to and now they have you to make fun of as well."

It was hot and the sleepy hour was creeping up. Nick wondered how he would ever find his way on his own as Leah guided him through the streets. He found it difficult to drive and watch out for the women moving slowly down the narrow channels with bread under their arms until they disappeared into doorways.

Outside the village they traced a stream along the bottom of the valley – it was the first time Nick was able to take his eyes off the road. Leah had pulled her feet up onto the seat and curled up against the door. There was something compelling about her, something warm and languid, but he couldn't help but think that she compared so unfavourably to her sister.

About half a kilometre down the road, Leah pointed:

"The house is up there." Nick looked, but couldn't see the top; the slope was almost perpendicular. "Here," she directed Nick across a precarious concrete slab laid over the stream. The road immediately began to climb and curve. "Keep to the right after the next hairpin." Leah didn't seem worried, so Nick didn't see why he should be. "There is more than one road up," Leah sounded jokingly philosophical, "but there is only one way down."

"That's comforting to know," Nick said grinding the gears as he tried to shift down while keeping the car moving.

"If you do get lost, you can ask anyone for the house by name, the people around here call it Bagni dei Diavoli."

Given the condition of the road up the hillside, Nick was expecting a modest home, but when the dirt turned to pavement and they passed through a monumental gate, he was still hardly prepared for the sight of the big villa. The deep burgundy masonry of the buildings and the manicured gardens and trees around the foreyard heartened him, despite the sense that he was walking into the lion's den. When he cut the engine there was a delightful trickling of water and saccades buzzing. For a moment, it made him think he was elsewhere. Then he jumped at the unmistakable sound of a sports car starting up just behind him.

"Nervous?" Leah laughed.

"Should I be?" Nick said, spying the red hood of an Alfa Romeo in the mirror.

"That depend's on how badly you want your contract changed."

"I thought I was coming by a little family business not being shown who was the poor cousin."

Leah smiled, as though she had said too much. She put

a hand on his wrist: "Daddy won't talk business with you today." Nick felt strangely relieved; he might even enjoy himself.

He got out stretching his legs and slowly turned around. The three boys from the bar were in the Romeo. The roof was down and the blond boy, Dino, smiling as always, was in the back sitting up on the trunk. Rachel was standing beside the car flirting with them; the driver revving the engine as though about to go but just waiting on a kiss and the hope of a squeeze. Rachel was dragging it out. Her dark church suit gone, replaced with a sun dress – light green against her olive skin.

Nick adjusted the shoulder strap of his bag. For some reason, it seemed heavier now. Leah was staring at her sister and the boys. He would have asked which way, but the car was making too much noise. "Over here," she said into his ear, "you'll be staying in the guest house," and she guided him by the elbow in her slow steps toward a large covered terrace on the far side of the grounds. She walked a little stooped, but still brandished her magnanimous smirk. The pitch of the sports car engine suddenly became piercing, and they turned to see the boys waving, but Rachel had already turned her back on them and was coming over.

"I'll take him," Rachel told her sister and Leah immediately broke off.

"Until later," Leah touched Nick's arm as she went.

"Your bag, let me," Rachel tried to lift it off Nick's shoulder.

"I'm fine," he resisted her tug, but knew he would have to give in because of the embarrassment of pulling her close to him.

"Just give me the thing," she laughed and added, "You pack light."

"I didn't expect to be staying long."

"If you need something, there are shops in Lucca. You'll have to go to Florence, though, for anything decent."

"Your father thinks I'll be staying a while?"

"Yes, he assumed you would," Rachel said with convincing innocence.

"I didn't bring a bathing suit," Nick said. They were coming up on a swimming pool.

"These are the old baths," Rachel skipped up the steps to the long narrow pool. "Daddy's a real swimmer. I think that's why he bought the place. There used to be stone seats in the water that divided up the pool."

"Into different classes?"

"Into the different temperatures."

"It's a shame they're gone," Nick said.

"I think so too, but the baths hadn't been used in almost a hundred years. Daddy really saved the place. The seats are still here." She showed him the big worn stone benches positioned like booths around the pool each sprouting an oleander.

Rachel took him by the arm and pointed: "Your room's down here."

At first Nick saw only the big covered terrace, then he noticed a stairway leading to an upper level with a line of windows looking out over the grounds and the valley.

As they were climbing the stairs, Rachel asked, "Nick, you have a company in Toronto, a computer company?"

"Yes, like your father's." He kept looking straight ahead – there was no railing.

"I'd like to visit. I was born there, you know."

"This was the laundry," Rachel said. As they reached the top she stepped aside to let Nick go in first. "The lower level was the bakery. You'll see the ovens around the back." The room was large and furnished with over-stuffed sofas and chairs and a bed with a monstrous hand-carved headboard. The ceiling sloped down sharply to the row of small windows he had seen from the outside. He went over and leaned his head out. An athletic looking woman in a maid's uniform was walking across the yard to the villa.

"That's Sandra," Rachel said from the next window.

"She doesn't look very happy."

"No. I'm tempted to say it's because she has to do your room, but that's not the only reason."

"Come," Rachel said holding out her hand to Nick, "I want to show you something." A door on the other side of the bedroom led to a small terrace and grotto which hung out over the valley. A plaque with a Latin inscription caught his eye and Rachel spoke up to explain.

"It says, 'St. Catherine bathed here.'" She tugged him by the arm and said, "Listen." There was a trickle of water coming from behind the statue of St. Catherine. "This is the spring that feeds the baths." She was still holding him by the hand, but when she let go, he took her by the shoulders and kissed her.

Rachel pulled away. "I'll see you later then. I imagine father will have you over for a drink before dinner."

Nick watched her fly through the door and disappear into the room.

Despite the sun at noon, it had turned cold by evening when Nick walked over to the house. He hadn't brought all that much to wear and hoped that the dark shirt and tie he had thrown together with the ususal linen jacket would pass – he regretted not having brought something more formal and something warmer. When he arrived in the big room, he had been tempted to curl up on one of the seats set into either end of the fireplace.

"That will take the chill off." Perchin rubbed his hands together and threw a small piece of wood onto the fire.

Nick saw Sandra, fit as a ballerina, standing perfectly still behind Perchin. It was she who had been sent to fetch him. All she had said was, "They're expecting you," and, "They dress for dinner." Nick stared at the wide marble hearth laid in checkerboard black and white squares. When Perchin finally turned, around he found her holding two wine glasses – her fists tightly clenched.

Nick heard ruffling in the recesses as Perchin excused himself to, "Bring down Veronica." It was Leah making the noise, getting comfortable on an ottoman; she was wearing a long dusty-red knit thing that she flipped over her feet – it set off her glasses. She saluted Nick with her wine, then had to prop herself up a little to take a sip.

"Would you like to put on some music?" She seemed to be asking more than offering. "Something for the occasion, I suppose. There's a pile of chant and polyphony there. Daddy collects the stuff."

Perchin's wife appeared. She was in a long white dress that draped from her shoulders in a big "V" and was belted at the waist like a classical Greek gown.

"Ah, Nick," Perchin arrived behind her. Nick was relieved.

"Nick was finding us some music," Leah spoke up from the ottoman.

"Please, please go ahead," Perchin pointed Nick back to the console and took his wife to a seat.

She was sitting up on the edge of her chair when Nick

came to join them. Before he got completely into his own seat, she asked: "What relationship exactly did your mother have with my husband?"

The first few strident chords of Stravinsky's *Firebird* burst across the room.

"Someone must have had that turned up," Leah said in a tone that could only have been reserved for Rachel.

"I'm afraid that was me," Perchin said on his way to turn it down, "I have a little passion for some old church music."

Nick waited until Perchin sat down again, then turned to Veronica: "You were asking about my mother."

She looked at Nick, as though he had suddenly changed the subject.

"Veronica," Perchin cut in, "you know Nick's mother. We visited in Toronto."

"Oh, yes, that's right, you reminded me – when you said Nick was coming – the woman with the dog and the apartment overlooking the water."

"Yes, my mother keeps me up-to-date, Nick," Perchin was tapping his fist, "I hear about you and your mother regularly."

Veronica looked like she wanted to question Nick further, but Perchin kept on. "What do you think of our village, Nick? Did you like the church?"

"I did. It has . . ."

"What is Nick's mother's relationship to Grandma?" Rachel cut in.

"Cousins, Sweetheart, cousins," Perchin looked behind him. Rachel had come in the other door. "Why don't you pull up a chair?"

Rachel stood between her parents, as though she were expecting more of an answer. Her idea of formal was somewhat simpler than the rest of the Perchins: a long light skirt and blouse with dangling earings to match her emerald.

"First cousins?" she asked.

"Second, I should think," Perchin said slowly and looked up at his daughter, clearly wondering why she was interested.

"What does that make us?" she asked her father, but she was looking at Nick.

When no one answered, Leah spoke up, "You and me and Nick? We're probably not anything."

"Sure you are," Perchin said, "you are blood relatives."

Nick could see them all looking at him, his dark hair, dark eyes, neutral skin, wondering if there was any resemblance, and concluding there was not.

Veronica, still on the edge of her chair, sucked in a slow breath: "What is it you want of my husband?" Her tone was lamenting, but her words accusing.

Nick looked at Perchin, hoping he would intervene. Perchin opened his mouth, "It's a – it's a . . ."

Veronica looked at her husband as though thunderstruck.

"It's just a little business, dear. We've both ended up dealing with the same company, amazingly enough, so I invited Nick over to work on the details, so we could get to see him."

Veronica turned to Nick; she now wanted to hear his side of the story.

Nick thought it best to adopt Perchin's "all is copasetic" tone, even though Perchin had lied about the coincidental nature of their working with the same company: "Just here to discuss a few fine points about the contract." It was a difficult one for Nick to swallow, given how hard Perchin must have worked to pull all the right strings to do the deal.

Veronica leaned back in her chair, tilting her head up: she seemed in pain. Rachel didn't take any notice of her and Leah was dreamily listening to the music. Perchin seemed concerned, but strangely powerless to console her.

"What does your company do, Nick?" Rachel asked, she came around to the other side of her mother's chair and sat on the arm next to Nick. The mother placed a hand in the daughter's lap and Rachel stroked her mother's cheek.

"It's a consulting company, data management consulting."

Nick thought Rachel was not listening – she and her mother were smiling at each other – but Rachel slid down the arm of the chair toward him, tapped his shoulder and said: "Just like Daddy's. How strange. How many employees do you have?"

The wary father turned his ear to his youngest daughter, his expression said he didn't think she ever would have given a damn about Nick's company.

"Twenty-five," Nick said tentatively. It was give or take a few depending on the week.

"Oh, so your company is bigger than Daddy's?"

"No, I hardly think so."

"It must be. All Daddy's got is Leah, Riccardo and a cleaning lady."

Clearly this was meant as a gibe. Perhaps to get Perchin to reveal something about his business. Rachel put on a triumphant little smile, "Well?" she asked, but Perchin wasn't biting.

Veronica suddenly sat up in her chair and addressed Nick, "Are you single?" Everyone's eyes were on her again and Nick wasn't sure if it was because she had sat up stiffly or because of what she had asked.

Nick didn't answer.

"Yes, he is," Perchin spoke for him, "I have it from Mother. I think that occupies much of our mothers' little chats, 'When is Nick going to find the right girl?'"

Rachel stood and nudged Nick's shoulder with her hip, "I'm sure Nick must have a girlfriend or two back in Toronto."

Nick still thought it best to hold his tongue and Rachel graciously changed the subject and started asking questions about Toronto. Clearly, she felt an affinity for her birthplace, and though, as she said, she couldn't remember it, she had collected a lot of anecdotes: the Danforth, Kensington Market, and the Beach. They got onto discussing the Japanese Garden in High Park and Rachel looked like she might ease her way down onto the arm of Nick's chair.

"Rachel, darling," her father cut in, "would you mind helping me move your mother up to the fire. She's a little cold."

"Nick," Perchin said, leaving Rachel to sort out Veronica's cushions and her throw, "if you like Stravinsky, Leah is the expert."

Nick hadn't really considered that the Stravinsky could have belonged to Leah, but now that Perchin clued him in, it did make sense. Nick had flipped through a collection of Milhaud, Poulenc and other contemporaries of *Les Six* – they must be Leah's too – and so he stood up beside Perchin and asked Leah about Stravinsky. She was well informed. It was a pleasure to see her animated, if only intellectually. Stravinsky she portrayed as self-absorbed and asinine; Satie, a little twisted. Perchin stood behind,

"Yes, yes," he agreed. He dragged up a chair and with a hand on Nick's shoulder pushed him into it. "You need a refill," he said scooping up Nick's glass. Leah got on to discussing the American composers and here Nick was lost with Leah throwing out names he had never heard of before. He drifted off as he listened and watched Sandra come spritely through the doorway with two large goblets in her hands – Perchin overseeing. Leah talked on – senile music teachers were popping into her conversation every-where.

"Please, let me," Nick meant to take the glasses from Sandra, but a stern look from Leah stopped him. From where she lay half reclining on the ottoman, she opened a hand for Sandra to pass her the glass and in so doing Sandra had to perch over Nick in a compromising way. Leah's smirk seeped back into her cheeks.

"Nick," It was Veronica's unmistakable hard voice, "are you Catholic?" She was standing at her chair facing him.

"What does it matter if he's Catholic?" Leah cut in swinging her feet off the ottoman.

Perchin looked suddenly fiery-eyed standing behind his wife, Nick wasn't sure if he was reacting to an affront against his wife or an attack on the church from his eldest daughter.

Leah stood up. "Honestly, with all the paedophiles cropping up everywhere, it's a wonder anyone wants to be a Catholic at all." She looked away when she spoke, as though she were engaging some phantom in the wall.

"No," Perchin spoke slowly, "no, it is important to be Catholic," his voice was so reasoned and quiet it hardly sounded like him.

Veronica still standing turned her piercing stare on her

husband, and in a low voice spoke the word, "Yes," she drew it out endlessly and as it undulated Nick garnered her meaning: "Tell Nick why, if he wishes to be part of us, he must be Catholic." But in the way Perchin recoiled, Nick wondered if he couldn't read another message in Veronica's single word: "Claus, do tell us why it is you make us suffer the Church so."

Perchin spoke up, but to Leah not to his wife: "Yes, it is important, it is of immense importance," his voice grew less tentative, "it is a matter of commitment, not to the Church but to yourself. It's a matter of identity, self-knowing through commitment to your own values."

"If that's what's so important about it," Leah bit into her words. She was facing her father now, but wouldn't raise her eyes above his feet. "What does it matter if I'm Catholic? I could be a Buddhist."

"Leah," Perchin tried to sound conciliatory, "the day you become a good Buddhist, I will beg your forgiveness."

"'Do unto others as you would have them do unto you,' I apply that." Leah looked at her father in a dodgy sort of way.

"I agree, Leah, you do."

Veronica collapsed into her chair with a lyrical sigh. All the Perchins stopped to look at her, but Leah and her father quickly resumed their positions. Through all this Rachel and Nick had slowly backed away until they stood shoulder-to-shoulder; neither of them wanting to appear to be taking sides. It was Perchin who spoke first: "This is the real world. It is easy to justify acting with aggression. The Church teaches you have to accept . . ."

"Oh, 'accept, accept,' the Church just wants everyone to be meek so they can control them. I treat people the way I want to be treated, no more, no less."

There was an scratching noise and everyone jumped from the tension: it was Sandra propping open the heavy dining room doors. Rachel stepped forward, as though into the vacuum: "Why don't we all turn the other cheek for a little kiss and go into dinner." She swung round ceremoniously and took Nick's head in her hands and kissed him on the cheek. Arm-in-arm they moved toward Sandra.

Leah came up behind them so quickly, Nick had a sudden fright. Leah whispered: "You're such a godamn good Catholic girl."

Rachel tried to laugh it off, but Nick could tell she was hurt. Then she spoke up for everyone to hear, "'Do unto others as you would have them do unto you.' Didn't someone say, 'even the Pharisees do as much.'"

Nick was awakened the next morning by the sound of water lapping against the hull of a boat. Where was he? The light coming in the row of windows suggested to him for a moment portholes, but, as his eyes cleared, he saw they were square and a little too big and he remembered where he was. He stumbled across to one of them and there was Perchin doing his morning laps in a mechanical freestyle: his body rocking evenly as each arm came out of the water momentarily pausing to syncopate the stroke while he glided the extra distance. Back at the bedside table, Nick grabbed his watch: six-fifteen. Quickly he looked for some clothes and hurriedly buttoned his shirt. He'd surprise Perchin coming out of the water. If Nick could catch him off-guard with a few pointed questions, perhaps Perchin would have to admit something about his real intentions of trying to take over Nick's business. At the doorway, Nick realized he was in a panic and knew he had to get a hold of himself. He stood in the shadow at the top of the stairway watching Perchin and listening to the smooth, even, regular sound.

Nick went quickly down the stairs trying not to make so much noise that Perchin might hear. Half way down he stopped, dashed back up to the room and took one of the magazines and a bottle of water that had been left for him. On the way back down, he told himself to breathe deeply, combed his hair back with his fingers and practised a relaxed smile.

As far as he could tell, he made it to the bench closest to the pool without Perchin noticing. The morning air was fresh. Under the umbrella, he flipped the pages afraid to glance over lest Perchin should see him looking. From the sound, he could tell Perchin hadn't lost a stroke moving face down in his impeccable style. Nick heard a bicycle take off over the driveway – it was Sandra all decked out in a racing suit; she looked determined. Nick nursed the bottle of water, waiting. It was almost empty by the time Perchin popped up goggle-faced beside him.

"Nick," Perchin sounded delighted, he flew up onto the side of the pool, effortlessly it seemed, but Nick knew Perchin was making a point.

"Are you coming into town with me?" Perchin went for a towel. He wiped off his watch to check the time. He was wearing one of those skippy Brazilian style suits.

To Nick the message was: "It's great you are an early riser too, we will work well together." Perchin twirled the towel into a roll to dry his back.

Nick cleared his throat and tried to sound confident. "Rachel promised to take me into Castelnuovo this morning. Perhaps, we could meet up this afternoon, after lunch."

"Sure, I agree," Perchin's face fell, but he quickly caught himself and smiled again patting Nick on the back, "you should get to see the place." He grabbed a robe off a chair. "There's breakfast for you in the house." He was off in his determined steps barely stopping to slip his feet into his sandals. In two strides he had the robe pulled on – it hardly covered his bum – a wildly coloured but faded psychedelic thing with a hood. It could have been from the 1960s.

Nick didn't make it into the office in Lucca that day or the next or the next, but on the morning of the fourth day he woke to find someone sitting on his bed. He thought it was Rachel and ran his hand up her arm only to open his eyes and find Leah's big glasses staring back at him. "What's that?" he asked. Leah was holding a steaming coffee, he could smell the hot milk.

"It's a start to a day at the office."

"I made plans with Rachel," he was about to add "sorry" in a sarcastic voice – three days with Rachel would make any man over-confident – but Leah cut him off.

"Cancelled," she said and in the way she said it he thought he had better go along with her. So this was how curly head handled his dirty work. Perchin had left on a business trip on the overnight train. He had spent most of dinner asking too polite questions about their day in Sienna.

Leah tore the sheet off him. She had guessed rightly – he was naked. She handed him the coffee, smiling, then kissed her finger tips and pressed them to his cheek. "We leave in half an hour."

Nick hadn't taken seriously Rachel's jibe about Perchin

only having Leah, Riccardo and a cleaning lady to work for him, but he realized her words were not far from the truth. When he got into the crowded ground-floor office on a side street in Lucca, he quickly learned to stay clear of Sophia, Perchin's dour secretary, who really did double as the cleaning lady because of Perchin's paranoia over security. Behind Sophia and her boxes and her files were two large offices, both immaculate and both could have been Perchin's, but one belonged to Riccardo Calveri, a slight and suave multilingual man with a moustache who dressed casually and one could have just as easily imagined standing in a vineyard. Leah's office, where she did the books, was down the hall by the lavatory: a windowless cell whose threshold no one ever crossed; both because Leah made it clear that visitors were not welcome lest they disturb the sea of paper that flew in a vortex every time the front door opened and also because there was nowhere to sit.

Nick was put in a bare office in an annex across the alley. A number of accountants and auditors came and went from here, but the only regular occupants were a couple of tight-lipped contract lawyers who came every day in their ties and ate their lunches at their desks. Everyone in the annex acted on specific instructions from Riccardo and understood they were to keep to themselves. After Nick's first session with Riccardo he saw why.

Riccardo had called him over to his office after letting him stew on his own for a couple hours with nothing to do but review two thin contracts with small consulting companies. Nick hardly had to read them: they were so remarkably similar to his own. When he finally got in to see Riccardo, Nick had to wait out the man's telephone conversation with endless time to marvel at the uncommon reddish hue of his long wavy mustache and how it seemed to curl over the receiver. When he was free, Riccardo had come round and greeted Nick with deference taking his hand with both of his, offering Nick coffee, something to eat, a drink, as though Nick by association with Perchin were somehow the superior. When Nick declined, Riccardo immediately returned to his desk and got down to the business at hand. He had a list of small tech companies in Toronto and started with the ones with which Nick had done business. He wanted to know who ran them, what their reputation was and who were their major clients. While Riccardo took notes, Nick wandered around the office mulling over the cases of antique daggers mounted on the walls and thought about the former colleagues in Toronto he had befriended.

Over the next few weeks, Nick got onto a first name basis with the two contract lawyers. They insisted on referring to him as Perchin's nephew, however many times he corrected them. They would not talk business, but Nick at least got them to talk about their children. The days went by with Nick not quite sure of his role, offering up whatever information he had, or could find through his contacts, playing the pampered nephew and going with Rachel to executive lunches from which he would, just as often as not, not return. He was anxious about his company at first, but his staff now took all their direction from a European auto-parts manufacturer. His old clients, with whom he had curried favour for years, were now all gone or perhaps disbursed without his knowledge to other companies on a long leash tugged by Perchin.

To get away from it all Nick planned to take Rachel away for a day to Milan. They were to catch an early show and come back on the train. He watched Perchin leave the pool that morning at the ususal time and gave him another twenty minutes to clear out; then Nick headed over to the house. He just caught sight of Sandra heading down the drive on her bike perched over the handlebars for her morning ride through the hills. When he reached the second floor, Leah was standing at her bedroom door: "Excellent, you're up early." It was Leah's job to hang around and bring Nick into Lucca. She tugged her nightgown up over her breasts, a little belatedly.

"Don't think I'll be in today," Nick said and headed up to the third floor. "Rachel," he called, knocking softly on her door.

"Oh, Nick is that you? I'm . . . I'm not ready, I think there is another train in a couple hours we can get."

On his way down, he encountered Leah again: "Coffee by the pool?" she asked.

Nick didn't say no: he had been meaning to have a talk with Leah anyway. To ask her advice, not in so many words, but to get a sense from her if Rachel would go away with him, perhaps back to Toronto. And if she did, what Perchin would do about it. Nick waited for Leah in the kitchen and set about putting on some coffee. He heard someone scrambling down the back stair and thought for sure it wasn't Sandra and definitely not Veronica. Then Leah standing behind him in her bathing suit said: "Is that Dino Calveri sneaking out the back again?"

Nick jumped for the door and was just in time to see Dino's blond head disappear around the corner of the villa.

"Is he Riccardo's son?" Nick asked.

Leah didn't say anything.

His heart began to pound and his hands shook. Nick thought he should not let on to Leah how disturbed he was but at the same time he knew it was futile. He went back into the kitchen and took down a cup as though to continue with the coffee but impulsively smashed it on the counter top.

After an awful silence Leah said, "What the hell," and she finished with the coffee.

Nick was grateful for her attitude even if she was only putting it on for his sake, it was a diversion he needed. Nick followed a little sheepishly behind her. His mind, as though avoiding the dilemma at hand, automatically began reviewing the lines he had rehearsed to bring up with Leah the idea of going away with Rachel. As he stepped into the morning sun beating off the stones around the pool, the blood began to throb in his ears. He wanted to ask Leah why the fuck Dino was there, but he knew at the same time it was his fault. It was obvious that Dino had been the boyfriend when Nick arrived on the scene; it was Nick who had interfered. Instead of some carefully prepared words what came out was: "Do you think Rachel will leave with me?"

"What? Do you mean go back to Toronto with you?" Leah waited as though giving Nick an opportunity to deny that was what he meant, but he did not and then she said: "Good luck," as though the thought were preposterous. Then she recanted a little: "Look, I'm sure she would want to get out of here, don't we all? I wouldn't count on it."

At the edge of the pool Leah dropped her robe and rolled her hair up into an instant bun, jabbing it with a pin, then descended gingerly down the steps in her red one piece into the water. When submerged, she pushed her arms out in a single breast stroke keeping her head above the water, turned and came back, and stepped delicately out of the pool again. Nick thought she looked voluptuous in a freakish sort of way. She came over to his chair and sat in his lap and wrapped her arms around his neck. He wanted to soften to her but his jaw was set; he wanted to hit something.

Suddenly, Leah rolled on Nick's lap and looked toward the head of the driveway. Nick could not see anything, but, sure enough, a few seconds later Sandra appeared pumping hard to make it over the crest of the hill. She was beat. It was already getting hot and she left the bike against the first tree. Her hair had come loose and she tied it back again; her face was covered in sweat.

"Sandra," Leah waved her arm back and forth with uncharacteristic enthusiasm, "I need you to do something for me."

Sandra looked back with undisguised disgust and came at a crab's pace, stopping to stretch-out her legs against the corner of the house.

Leah pulled on Nick's arm, "Come on." She grabbed her robe and threw it over her shoulder. Then dragging Nick by the hand, she led him up the stairs to his room. Leah obviously had something in mind, and Nick went along with her, feeling confused: half distraught and half like he had an hour or two to kill before Rachel came down. Leah took him over to the bed and with an arm around his waist eased him onto his back. She just lay there against him listening. Nick pricked his ears up too, he could hear Sandra coming. She was taking her time up the steps. Leah had left the door wide open leaving the sun shine directly into the room. The wind too was moving through with most of the windows open. Nick watched the doorway in anticipation of Sandra appearing there, the dark outline of her tight suit against the sun, but what came through the door was the scent of her body, her perspiring body.

Leah rose up on her elbow, "Over here," she said, as though speaking to a child when Sandra appeared. Sandra took a feeble step toward them and Leah tapped the side of the bed and spoke with a sugary smile, "Come right up."

Sandra looked like she could kill, like she could have calmly wrapped her fingers around Leah's neck – and finally Nick realized that Leah had something over Sandra, something deadly. Sandra stepped up, though she might just as easily have spit in Leah's face, and Leah, smiling grandly, stood and lifted Sandra's arms straight over her head. Then in a single yank, pulled Sandra's top up till it covered her face – her breasts fell out. Leah guided Sandra down onto the bed between them. Nick was reluctant and intensely aware of the circle of those taking advantage, but he was angry, very angry.

In the days and weeks that followed Nick fully expected that Leah would hold the knowledge of their triangle over his head too, but she didn't. If anything, she softened, even became deferential toward him. As for Rachel, after an awkward day in Milan, things returned to normal. He told himself that he could rise above the Dino incident, but he knew he was simply infatuated and couldn't see straight. Nick was no closer to convincing Rachel to go away with him; and slowly he was coming round to thinking that to try to sway her would be unfair, Perchin had too strong a grip on her. In his lucid moments, Nick realized his options had narrowed and there was nothing left for him to do but confront Perchin.

One evening after working late in Lucca, Nick came across from the annex and tried the door, it opened –

someone was still there. He had stayed late on purpose, because he knew Perchin was expected back. Perchin's office door was open so he went in to wait. He figured Perchin would know what he had come about, he'd made so much trouble with Riccardo over getting his company back and wanting to go back to Toronto. At the same time, he and Rachel had become so inseparable that no one would have thought he would simply say good-bye and go.

"Looking for new office space?" It was Leah being her smirky self.

"That old priest from Valdottavo just about ran me down a minute ago when I crossed the street."

Leah laughed: "He's been a menace ever since Daddy gave him the Mercedes. If he shrinks anymore you won't be able to see the top of his head. Daddy can't be long then, he was meeting with the Padre." She slipped into her sweater and hitched her purse on her shoulder.

"You trust me alone in here?" Nick fully expected she would kick him out of her father's office and lock the door, or at least wait around with him until Perchin got back.

Leah kissed him and went to leave with her head down to hide her smile, as though she was revelling in the thought of her father's consternation when he arrived to find Nick in his office.

The display cases mounted on the walls in Perchin's office had old manuscript folios in them. Nick guessed they'd be pages from *The Prince*, but he found they were all renaissance manuscripts: designs for water pumps and olive presses.

"Nick, Nick, it is good to see you, I hardly know you are around these days." Perchin came right in. He was doing a good job of sounding sincere: Leah must have waited outside to warn him or maybe she just used a cellphone. He was going on about some new client, a car seat maker and intimating that he and Nick should go off to Germany to check them out.

Nick sat across the room waiting for Perchin to take a breath – he had practised trying to be blunt: "I'm going back to Toronto and Rachel's coming with me."

"You and Rachel having been spending a lot of time together."

Nick held his tongue; he did not want to get dragged into proving how close he and Rachel were.

"I won't tell you it's foolish, you've given this a good deal of consideration. I know you have, you're a thoughtful person." Perchin came out from behind his desk and sat in the big paisley arm chair next to Nick. "You've been conscientious in your own business dealings and in your work here with us, and I know you wouldn't be rash in how you treat my daughter. You need someone like you, you ought to have someone like you, someone who can appreciate that there is a little more to life. You know what I mean? Of course you do, what am I saying? "Leah's a thoughtful person. She's like you in that way."

Perchin stood and went for the credenza, "Drink?" he asked, not waiting on a "yes" or a "no." He dug to the back for a bottle. Nick had never noticed the cabinet before and he wondered why. "Water?" Perchin held the glass of liquor in one hand and a decanter of water in the other.

"Please," Nick said and watched Perchin's curly head tilt, as he tapped the decanter to the glass. It reminded Nick of the priest he had served as a boy, who would scrape the sweat from the porcelain water jug over the brim of the chalice to mingle the water and the wine. Perchin and he began to bicker politely over whether being thoughtful and intellectual made Leah like Nick, the glass in Perchin's hand appeared more and more to be filled with nothing but water.

Finally, Nick conceded: "Yes, Leah's like me."

"'. . . but . . ., but,' I'm sensing a 'but' here."

The pitch of Perchin's voice rose like an approaching car until Nick cut him off: ". . . but, we're not compatible."

Perchin slammed his glass on the desk: "Oh, take Leah, she's more like you."

Nick looked at his shoes, then at Perchin: "I'm taking Rachel."

"You can't just take Rachel, she's a girl. How do I know you won't dump her when you realize you can't talk to her because she's just a child?"

"She wants to go."

"She can't travel without my permission." Perchin stood up and shuffled about the office. "Besides, she wouldn't go anyway." Perchin sat and started going through his letters. He spoke out loud, as though Sophia were seated across from him: "File. Trash. Reply."

Nick spoke up: "I want my company back."

"Not till you fulfill the terms of your contract," Perchin continued sorting the letters.

"If I complete the contract, if I work for you . . ."

"Yes," Perchin stopped to listen.

". . . You'll give me back control?"

"Yes."

"How long?"

"How long will it take for you to fulfill the contract? That depends how fast . . ."

Nick leaned forward statue-like. It felt like something in his head would burst.

"Okay, I can give you a good idea of how long." Perchin began to mumble, "Twenty-two months for development, eighteen months . . ." The numbers were as Nick feared.

Perchin scribbled his calculations and looked up: "Eighty-four months."

Nick thought a moment: "Seven years. Okay, I'll complete the terms of the contract, but not here, I'll do it in Toronto, and I'm taking Rachel with me."

"Stay here." In two steps Perchin was around the desk again. He placed a hand on Nick's shoulder: "Work in Lucca where I can keep an eye on you."

"No," Nick was spitefull – all he could think of was the "eighty-four months."

"Have you bothered to ask Rachel what she wants?"

"Rachel's worried," Nick could not deny it. "She told me she loves you, but she said she doesn't want to end up like Leah, rotting away in a closet in Lucca." Rachel had never said as much, but Nick knew he had enough of the truth to get under Perchin's skin.

Perchin squeezed Nick's shoulder: "You want too much, Nick, you want too much. It's foolish, but if you're going to go away with Rachel, then you will have to marry her." Perchin seemed resigned and stared at the floor.

Not very many days later, Nick woke up in the humid morning Tuscan air – his eyes and face felt swollen. He tried to lift his head but his neck could hardly bear it, and when he tried to pull himself up with his arms he found they were rubber; one of them was under something. Was he sick? He must be convalescing; when he tried to move it felt like his body had been immobile for days. Finally, he managed to roll himself up on one elbow. A woman was seated up in bed with him; her legs were over one of his arms. The legs were heavy, not like Rachel's, then he recognized a hazy band of black across the woman's, Leah's eyes.

"He's awake," she said. There was someone else in the room.

Nick remembered the frustration of searching for Leah's dark glasses, the strain of looking through the people emerging from the house. He thought it was Rachel when he saw the wedding gown, then a second white gown. He couldn't tell which was which – the trees – the people streaming out, the laughing, he was searching for glasses, Leah's glasses – he couldn't tell – the demi-veils – he couldn't tell, because neither was wearing glasses. He should not have seen Rachel before the ceremony. But was it unlucky if he didn't know for sure which one was her.

He could feel someone hanging over him, hanging on his shoulder as he perched out on the window sill to stare down to the house: it was a man; he was so close Nick could feel his breath.

He remembered the voice: "We have to go out to the grotto." It was Riccardo, his appointed best man.

He remembered Riccardo tapping his face, tugging at his tie, the swipe of his lapels, Riccardo's weathered hand. They were waiting by the grotto. "A drink," Riccardo said, "for the nerves." A bottle of vodka tucked behind St. Catherine. "You're not smiling," Riccardo said and poured a second shot.

It was a hoard, a religious hoard. Everyone pushing up to the make-shift altar. The priest was speaking, mumbling, smiling. He had his back to them like he was saying a Tridentine mass. This is wrong, wrong, Nick thought; he had to give some order to this crowd. He began moving people about, Veronica to the back, Riccardo beside him, but no matter how he shuffled them, the crowd, amorphous, slithered as though with the turning of Perchin's eye. The only constant thing was that Rachel clung to one arm and Leah to the other. Nick kept Rachel in the corner of his eye; she seemed sad, beyond her St. Catherine, the water splashing over her face.

At the dinner table Rachel was less sad, though no less distracted: the long table stretching out with endless people, people from the church who talked at Nick in Italian. He tried to smile. Finally, he was free of Leah, circulating between courses. She was buoyant. Riccardo listened closely to all Rachel's *grazie*, she said little else. Cancello's daughters were flowing up and down the length of the table doubled handed with the wine. Old man Cancello himself hovering behind Nick and Rachel acting on the nods of Perchin, keeping the champagne flowing.

Nick did see Rachel stirred, a flash of emotion, when she disappeared in the darkness behind the guest house. Nick was following Riccardo, he didn't know why, but he followed the redness of his hair slipping through the dancers around the pool. He was biting his lip. Dino was walking into the trees, his arm around the shoulders of the old priest.

By the pool, Sandra was speaking into Nick's ear, "Dino needs to see her. You've got to help him." Her hand on Nick's back to stop him from slipping away. "It's not what you think. He's afraid he'll never see her again. Here comes Veronica. You must stop her." The worried delight on Rachel's face. Dino hanging on the corner of the guest house – his shirt was dirty.

"Veronica," Nick held his arms out to her, her half stiff, half listless stride, riding into his arms. He held her so that her dark eyes would not see Rachel slip down the side of the house into the trees.

"Don't fear, Nick, don't fear," Veronica spoke with the softness of a mother. "First you will be cheated, then you will be blest." He held her longer.

Beyond Veronica, while her words played again in his ear, Nick saw Leah checked by Sandra. The ineffectual struggle, a kick – Leah's face falling vanquished – Rachel and Dino must be together. Leah's white dress heaving in anger – her disgust. She walks away. She doesn't give a damn.

The white bodice rising up above him in bed is connected to Leah's heavy legs. All the sounds muffled in Nick's ears, Leah smoking, Leah talking, talking to someone – Riccardo – and another voice, a deep voice from outside. The door to St. Catherine's source is open.

The voice. Nick tried to sit up. The voice, that low drone: was it in his head? It sounded like it was coming from the grotto. Perchin? Nick scrabbled over Leah's legs. With one foot on the floor he fell. His head. Leah sniggered. Nick rolled over on the floor, he was naked. His engorged genitals slapped against his thigh. On his hands and knees he made for the door but fell again and pulled himself up on the wall. He pulled the door wide open. Perchin was with Rachel at the table. She was wearing Perchin's coloured bathing robe. The table was set with a magnificent bouquet of orchids, breakfast was spread all around it, a side table with fruit, champagne. Perchin looked up. Nick expected a deadly look. What came back was resignation, inevitability, pity, pity, yes, pity. Rachel had her hands cupped in her father's; she wouldn't look up.

Perchin stood and Rachel with him. He took her by the shoulders and they made a move to come in. Nick's head was clearing, he made it to the bed, but could only sit breathlessly; he didn't have the strength to cover himself. He wanted to cover himself, but he could only stare at the doorway, listening to the footsteps coming in. It was Sandra's hand that yanked the sheet out from under Leah and drew it across Nick's lap. Leah still smoking in bed; Riccardo was sitting in a chair by the windows in a corduroy suit and cravat. He was leaning to see around Sandra to continue his conversation. Perchin brought Rachel in, holding her shoulders in a two-fisted grip. They stopped in front of Nick. Rachel stared at Nick's feet, holding the threadbare robe tightly around her.

"Here is your contract." Perchin's voice was tired. The paper fell on the bed beside Nick, as he shuffled Rachel out.

Nick tried to focus on the lines, but he went nauseous. He lifted the paper; it looked like the same old contract he had come to Tuscany to get out of, but he couldn't read it. He flipped to a stiff page on the back and held it close to his face until the lines became clear: it was his certificate of marriage to "Leah Perchin."

Nick dragged himself over to the window. He was about to hurl insults down on Perchin's head, but all he saw was a large speckled billy goat clip-clapping along beside the pool with a tiny lamb. When he called Rachel's name, the lamb turned, its nose ring flashed green and she winked.

Printed in October 2005
at Gauvin Press Ltd., Gatineau, Québec